Her Mother's Voice

Anna Woo

To all mothers and daughters,

may you find peace after the struggle.

Chapter One

"Emily-a, give me call, it *important*," said the voice on the answering machine.

"Em..." the familiar voice cried out. Emily stood in her apartment after a long day of conducting assessments and pressed the skip button on her answering machine until no new messages appeared. Emily-a! She heard her mother's voice in her head calling her. Her pronunciation never changed in intonation or tone, except to get louder. Emily-a! She said her name out loud with a Chinese accent. She always thought it was funny how her mother changed English names into Chinese sounding ones just by adding the letter "a." Friends,' neighbours,' even strangers' names became more Chinese-like. Accepted. For example, Debby became "Debby-a," Charlie became "Charlie-a," Cindy became "Cindy-a" and so on. It even made it easier for her mom to talk or gossip about that person too!

But why does she keep calling? Four messages! Her mother was always a worrywart, but ever since Dad died of a heart attack a year and a half ago she seemed more on edge, calling daily to tell her about her health ailments and dispensing advice about foods, medicines, dangers on Toronto streets – whatever Ma heard about. Emily tried to listen patiently; after all, Dad was no longer around to be Ma's sounding board. Her repetitive lectures irritated Emily, reminding her of the fighting she escaped from when she left home for school.

"Daddy, Daddy," she said with a sigh as she stroked the framed family picture she kept beside the answering machine. It was taken at Christmas 1985; the only picture she had of herself as an adult with her parents. She picked it up from the top of her Ikea bookshelf, turned around to face her white dining room table and settled down into a matching chair. Dad stood to her right in the picture. His eyes were bright, happy. Healthy. *Not that Dr. Eng, the stupid family doctor, would know any better!* She had called Dr. Eng and questioned him about her dad's visit to him the day before his coronary episode. Dad hadn't been his usual energetic self. Ma said he was grumbling about having stomach pain, nausea, dizziness and teeth pain. Dr. Eng just sent him home to "rest" and "take it easy." He brushed her concerns away and took his usual all-knowing attitude, assuring Emily that he had checked Dad out, and everything was "fine." Dad suffered a heart attack that night. After he died, Emily tried in vain to get her mother to change doctors. She hated that arrogant man who let her father die. Her mother would just shake her head and say, "He is like family, Emily."

Emily was just as tall as her dad and they stood shoulder to shoulder in the picture like equals. She thought of him as her ally against Mom, but he never openly opposed her mother. Emily found she couldn't complain about Ma to him – Dad would screw his face up like he was eating something sour if she tried that.

She missed him and obviously her mother did too. Her stomach growled, and she got up to put the picture back in its place. It was 5:30. Ma would be cooking dinner. She walked past the phone and into the kitchen.

In the kitchen, she pulled out the rice cooker her mother had bought for her when she was leaving for university eight years ago.

"This way you won't burn the rice," Ma had cautioned in Chinese.

"Thanks a lot," she said to her and pushed the gift aside. Secretly, she was thankful for the gift. She did know how to cook rice or at least she thought she did.

Now she rinsed the grains of rice several times under cold water, like her mother had shown her. Scratches like scribbled messages lined the bottom of the pot. It had been well used. She scrubbed at the wet grains, creating a cloud over the clear water. After the fourth scrub, she let the rice lay still, hiding messages below. With a flat palm, she checked the water level before closing the lid and turning the rice cooker on. She was an expert now, but had been a bit cocky during her first year of school, dismissing her mother's instructions and doing things her way. She invited her new friends for dinner and cooked a classic rice dish her mom would make at home. No one at her dinner party complained about the crunchy texture of the rice, and she pretended not to notice. Of course, she was dying inside. *How could she not know how to make rice?* She learned to not overfill the pot, ensuring the correct rice to water quantities.

She opened the fridge and took out mushrooms, onions and broccoli for dinner. Her piece of red meat had thawed in the sink and she cut it into thin slices.

Thank God it's Thursday, sighed Emily, as she covered her mouth in mid-yawn. Her hands clasped the back of her head and she rolled her neck slowly from side to side and stared at her business card magnet on the fridge: Emily Chow, B.Sc. OT., Occupational Therapist. Emily dropped these cards off like candy to clients, as she liked how everyone seemed to pop them automatically on their fridge. "So much still to do!" she groaned out loud as she thought about the files in the spare bedroom, her office, piled neatly on the computer desk. She liked to get her reports out within a week of assessing a client so that the information was still fresh in her mind. She knew that this made her popular with many companies and she had a very busy schedule lined up for the next six months. Three more reports to churn out to take care of the previous week's assessments. Emily smiled as she stir-fried the vegetables and meat. She kept Fridays free so that she could catch up on her report writing and start to unwind for the weekend.

"Happy anniversary, happy anniversary, happy anniversary, happy anniversary," she sang as Friday was her one year anniversary date with her boyfriend Sam. Emily licked her lips as she remembered the raw oysters she last had at Touché, their favourite restaurant. They were going again tomorrow. *Will I order oysters?* Hungry, she turned off the stove and grabbed her favourite dark blue Japanese bowl. She scooped two servings of rice into it and topped the rice with the steaming food.

Pouring herself a glass of iced tea, she walked into the dining room and pushed her right elbow into the power button of the stereo also on the bookshelf, before sitting down to eat. Sweet garlic, onions and soy sauce filled her mouth and she sang out loud to familiar radio tunes between bites. She was enjoying her meal when she heard a voice call out, prompting her to lower the volume of the stereo.

"Emily-a, it's Ma."

She felt the hair at the back of her neck tingle and she stopped eating.

"You home? Everything okay? Please call!" Ma spoke in a combination of English and Chinese, but tended to speak only in Chinese whenever she was anxious or angry. Emily spoke only in

5

English. She could speak Chinese, but after all these years of not using it, she felt stupid whenever she tried.

Emily glanced at the red light flashing from her answering machine. Five messages now. *What is up? God, these complaints are getting tiring!* She picked up her chopsticks and bowl and shovelled the remaining food, then downed her drink. She looked at the clock again: 6:15. *Let's get it over with.* She picked up the phone and dialed.

"Ma, it's me," she said. "Why do you keep calling?" she asked impatiently.

"It important!"

"What?"

"The doctor, you know Dr. Eng, ask me come in."

"So?"

"So you come home take me see doctor. He want *you* come too!"

Emily sighed out loud. "Ma, I have to work you know."

"What work so important? More important than mother?"

Emily squeezed her free hand into a fist. *Guilt.* It always worked. Ma knew how to get what she wanted. *How can she say that?* That familiar anger rumbled inside of her. She felt like a teenager again. *Trapped.* She stared at the gleaming whiteness of her knuckles while her mother went on about not feeling well. They didn't get along the way typical mother and daughters do. She couldn't confide in Ma or tell her anything without being lectured. *What does she know about my life anyways?* "Okay, okay, what time is the appointment?" She finally relented.

"Eleven o'clock tomorrow."

"Fine, I'll see you in the morning." She hung up before her mother had a chance to say anything else. Taking her mother to the doctor shouldn't be a big deal, and yet it was the duty associated with it that made it a chore. A burden. *When would she be free of it?* Fueled by adrenaline she grabbed her dishes, marched into the kitchen and washed them quickly. *Daddy, Daddy, where are you now?* Daddy. She got that name from television, maybe from *The Brady Bunch*? Daddy was the sweets man, the one who gave her gifts to bribe her into being a "good girl" who didn't fight with Ma. He was a buffer between the two of them, but now he was gone, leaving only friction. She threw the dishtowel down. It was just like before or maybe it's just like it's always been? Drained, she poured herself a glass of cold water and sipped it down. It was 7:00 and she had more work to do now that she has lost tomorrow morning. Emily exhaled, walked into her office and turned the computer on. She rolled her shoulders back and started typing.

Morning was bright. Warm heat was awakening the ground, allowing for shoots of greens to rise. Some yellow faces had opened, warming the front entrance of Emily's apartment building. Others stayed closed; colours to be discovered. Emily drove from her apartment in Toronto to her parent's home in Oakville. Traffic was sparse and she managed a fast 20-minute drive. She turned her car up the black slope and parked in front of the red garage door. "Red for luck," Ma had said. It stuck out like a sore thumb amongst the predominantly gray and brown garage doors. *Hate it still.* She cringed as she walked past and used her key to let herself in.

"Emily-a, have some soup," called her mother as soon as she entered. "I made for you last night."

"I'm not hungry."

Emily kicked her shoes off and placed them on the plastic mat. She preferred the pink embroidered slippers to the red pair and slipped them on. Brown, green and yellow flip flops also lined up against the wall awaiting movement. All guests were required to remove their shoes and had the option of wearing an indoor shoe if they liked. Her pretty slippers clicked softly as she walked across the yellowing linoleum and into the kitchen. Ma was standing in front of the brown stove with a ladle in her hand.

"Ma, it's too early for soup!" She groaned as she sat down at the kitchen table.

"It good for you," said Ma as she filled a red bowl with steaming broth and placed it in front of Emily.

Emily stared down at the white square pattern that bordered the brown kitchen table. The plastic finish that protected the table was scratched, but it still felt smooth as she ran her finger along the design, pretending to draw. *How often had she sat at this exact spot drinking soup?* Soup was always "good for you," and it didn't matter if you liked it or not, were hunger or not. It was meant for your health and taken like medicine.

"'Ai-ya drink up!" said Ma.

Annoyed, Emily grabbed the soupspoon and blew down on the hot bowl. The blue dove on her soupspoon had faded and the Chinese character was difficult to see. She dipped into the soup and tasted watercress. *Mmm, it was a good soup.* Comforted, she slurped it down happily. Food was the only bond she and her mother really shared. Ma cooked all the time – no canned or frozen stuff was allowed in their house when she was a kid. She ate rice at almost every meal with different kinds of Chinese cuisine like stir-fried vegetables, black-bean ribs, steamed fish, oven roasted barbeque pork and, of course, homemade soup. It wasn't like she loved every type of soup or every dish her mother cooked. In fact, as a teenager she avoided having meals at home for a short time so she could be like everyone else and eat pizza, wings and McDonalds. Emily was surprised to discover she preferred her mother's cooking to the junk food. This didn't stop her from eating it of course, but she did start to request certain dishes from her mother, especially when she came home from university. Ma was pleased by this and went out of her way to make Emily's favourites.

"Good soup, Ma," she said, now relaxed.

"Your favourite right? You want more?"

"No thanks. So what have you been doing this week?"

"Oh, playing Mahjong with your auntie and friends. You know how Auntie Sue like to win? She not win all week so play again tomorrow!"

Emily nodded and laughed. Her mother had one sister who lived nearby in town. Auntie Sue was a few years younger than her mother and one of her main supports. She looked at her watch: 10:45. "Ma, we'd better get going or we'll be late for your appointment."

"Okay, okay." Her mother took off her apron and picked up her purse.

"So why did you go to the doctor anyways?" asked Emily.

"Oh, I still have this cough – remember I mention to you at Chinese New Year?"

"Uh huh. But you seem better now, right?"

"Yes, not coughing much, but lots of stomach pain. Remember I tell you before?"

Emily tried to recall and thought maybe she mentioned having a stomachache or something in one of the phone calls, but her mother had an ulcer so she dismissed it.

"Dr. Eng call yesterday and say I better come in and bring you. I asked him why, but he just said you have to come in!" Ma said anxiously.

Emily looked down at her mother. Her petite frame came up to her shoulders and a familiar smell tickled her nose. Ma liked to wash her face with Noxzema. *Did she look thinner?*

"Something wrong – I tell you this before!" Ma complained.

Emily helped her mother with her coat. *Maybe she was a bit skinnier?* She touched her hair. It was still soft and black. Healthy.

"What you doing?" asked Ma.

"Oh, just looking at your hair."

"My hair good?" Ma asked proudly. "I am 65 and don't need to dye my hair. Everyone says I have good hair."

"Yes, you have good hair," Emily said, as she thought how healthy hair reflected good health. She smiled feeling reassured.

Emily drove through the familiar neighbourhood of her childhood, past two storey homes with long front yards and streets lined with old oak and maple trees. She made her way downtown to the medical building. In the parking lot, she took a ticket and parked her car.

"When did they start charging for parking here?" she asked.

"Oh, some time ago. Here let me give you money for the ticket." Ma put twenty into Emily's hand.

"Ma!" *She's always treating me like a child!* Emily tossed the money back at her mother. "I work now! I have money!"

They walked into the lobby of the medical building and took the elevator up to the third floor. Emily had her own doctor in Toronto and hadn't seen Dr. Eng professionally since high school. She was surprised to see the same fake wood counter of her childhood. Ma sat down and she took a seat beside her. Weathered-looking office chairs lined the square waiting room, and a double row of chairs, metal backs together, made a straight line in the middle of the room. A few seated patients were also waiting for Dr. Eng. She sighed; relieved to see Ma did not seem to know any of them.

"Old. Cheap," whispered Ma waving her hand across the waiting room.

"Shh," whispered Emily.

"Dr. Eng has so much money. You think he spend some to make this place nice," continued Ma.

Emily nodded in agreement, hoping to silence her mother. She despised the man, but didn't want to make fun of him in his own office. She reached over and picked up a magazine. It was a "Reader's Digest." Ten years old. *So, she's right.* Emily smirked and put it down.

Dr. Eng, a tall man in a white lab coat emerged. He called to the waiting patients and sent them to examination rooms. "Mrs. Chow," he said turning to face them. "Come in." Emily and her mother followed his coattail to his office. She felt on edge, realizing this was the first time she had to face Dr. Eng since her dad died.

"Just wait here," he instructed as he left, shutting the door behind him to attend to his other patients. Emily took a seat in one of the new tanned leather chairs. She looked at the framed pictures of Dr. Eng's adult children that faced her from his large oak desk. His daughter wore gold-rimmed glasses and her hair was pulled back from her wide face. His son did not wear glasses and was tall and thin like Dr. Eng.

"Dr. Eng's children very smart," said Ma. "Son is training to be doctor and daughter is a nurse."

"Smart, but not very attractive," Emily snapped. Dr. Eng had come to Oakville around the same time as Emily's dad did in 1958. She was unsure how they came to know each other, but he spoke Toisan, the same Chinese dialect that all the local Chinese residents spoke. Her dad spoke highly of Dr. Eng's achievements and intelligence, as he had to start over and study medicine in Canada to become a doctor. Every

Chinese person in town went to see Dr. Eng, and he received special attention from her parents and all their friends. Her dad even went over to his big house to mow the lawn for him one summer because he was asked to. *Some privilege!* Emily didn't understand why Dr. Eng deserved this, and she thought he enjoyed all the attention and advantages of his position just a little *too* much.

"Okay, see you next time," Dr. Eng called out to someone as he opened the office door and came in.

"Ah, Emily-a, you look so thin!" proclaimed Dr. Eng, as he took a seat at his desk. Emily resisted scowling and avoided his eyes. "Mrs. Chow," he said switching easily to Chinese for Ma.

"Dr. Eng," said Ma, immediately launching into a description of the soup she had made for Emily. Dr. Eng smiled. Emily noticed that his thin lips spread across his face, but he did not show his teeth. He spoke softly, agreeing with every comment Ma made, but his voice was smooth, arrogant. He laughed a bit too easily with Ma. *Fake.*

"Emily-a, where are you manners?" Ma asked suddenly.

Emily frowned at her mother. *Why did she do that?* "Dr. Eng," she said as she looked blankly at the doctor.

"Mrs. Chow, do you mind if I speak to Emily for a few minutes?" asked Dr. Eng.

"Sure, sure," said Ma and stood up.

"Just wait outside in the waiting room and I'll come back for you in a few minutes," Dr. Eng told her as he opened the door.

God, now what? Emily folded her arms against her chest.

Dr. Eng sat down and opened a file.

"Emily, I've got some bad news," he said as he stared at his file.

"About..."

"Well, there is no easy way to say this..."

She straightened up in her seat.

"Your mother has liver cancer. It's terminal. I'm sorry."

Emily gasped and tried to find her voice. *What did he just say?* She looked at Dr. Eng's face. He wasn't smiling.

"Your mother does not know exactly what is going on. She knows her ulcer acted up again. The new medication for the ulcer is working, and I believe the specialist has indicated it is resolving. So far I just told her there is still something else going on with her stomach and to eat well, get rest...you know how she worries, right?" He nodded his head as if Emily had responded.

"So...if you don't have any questions, I'll give her the news now, okay?" Dr. Eng stood up, walked past her and towards the door.

"Wait!" Emily shouted to get past the lump in her throat.

Dr. Eng stopped and turned around.

15

"Don't you think you could answer some questions for me? When did this happen? How did this happen?"

Dr. Eng sighed and scratched his head.

She stared at Dr. Eng, deafened by the pounding in her head.

"We are not sure how this happened. Cancer can happen to anybody. We just discovered it by accident because of her ulcer, so she is lucky really."

"Lucky? In what way? You said it is terminal. Does this mean Ma is going to d...die?" Her voice felt hoarse.

Dr. Eng came over to Emily and put his hand on her shoulder. "Look Emily, you have to be strong. This type of cancer is not easy to treat and in your mother's case, it is very difficult to treat. It's very advanced."

Emily shook Dr. Eng's hand off her shoulder. *Boom-boom, boom-boom.* The pounding of her heart grew louder. She gazed at Dr. Eng's moving mouth, uncertain of his words.

"As well," Dr. Eng said as he sat down on the corner of his desk to face her. "It looks like she may only have four weeks left."

Four weeks, oh my God! Cancer? Emily felt hot tears stream down her face. She turned away to hide from Dr. Eng.

"I'm sorry. Just make her comfortable, Emily, okay?" Dr. Eng said as he patted her on the shoulder and left the room.

Emily grabbed a fistful of tissues from the tissue box and blew her nose. She quickly brushed away the tears and tried to focus on the picture of Dr. Eng's kids to compose herself.

Dr. Eng appeared back at the door with her mother, and they took their seats.

Don't look at Ma. Don't look at Ma. She cleared her throat and blinked to concentrate on Dr. Eng.

"Mrs. Chow, I'm afraid I have some bad news for you." Dr. Eng began.

"Yes," said Ma sitting up in her seat.

"Well...I'm sorry to say, but it appears you have cancer."

"Cancer! I knew it! I knew I was dying!" Ma shouted and slapped Emily's arm, almost triumphant.

"Ma..." Emily managed.

"What? Oh," Ma said quieting her voice.

"What are we going to do?" Emily asked meekly.

Dr. Eng sighed and shook his head. "It's very advanced. I'm afraid there is little that can be done."

Emily shot a look at Ma. She was pouting.

"I've arranged for you to see a cancer specialist, Dr. Fung," Dr. Eng said. "He will take care of everything. You don't have to worry." Dr. Eng got up and patted Ma on the back. He handed Emily a business card.

"Can you take your mother to this appointment next week?" He asked her.

Without looking at the card, she nodded.

Chapter Two

Emily and Ma drove home in silence. She didn't know what to say or even how to comfort her mother. *It'll be okay* she imagined herself saying with a confident voice and a pat on the shoulder. That reminded her of Dr. Eng's fake performance, and she decided against it. She stole a glance at her mother. She was still pouting! That infamous expression her mother always used to show she was mad, angry, upset or right. Anytime Emily did something Ma didn't like or disapproved of that pout was there. Now guilt was added to the mix of emotions she was overwhelmed with. She wished she hadn't looked at her mother and drove steadily on.

Inside the house, her mother walked slowly into the family room and slumped down. She looked so thin and frail, reminding Emily of a small child. She knew she had to say something, but her mind was still at a loss. *Say something. Something!*

"Ma, you okay?" She finally managed.

Ma nodded and replied, "Tired."

"Why don't you go have a nap then?"

Ma agreed, and she helped her up the stairs to the bedroom, thankful she had found her some occupation. Once the door was closed hot tears sprang from her eyes, overwhelming Emily. She dashed down the stairs into the bathroom. Safely inside, she muffled the animal-like sounds that erupted from deep within her.

"Four weeks! This can't be happening!" She paced the bathroom floor. Her dad wasn't around to help her. She had no other siblings to rely on. Sure, she had experience playing adult roles for her mom in the past, like filling out forms, translating words into Chinese, mundane tasks that she learned to despise, but what was she going to do now? More tears threatened, when an image of a face flashed through her mind. *Yes.* Opening the bathroom door, she found the telephone and dialed her aunt's number.

Auntie Sue answered at once.

"It's Emily, Auntie Sue," she paused to steady her voice. "I'm at Ma's place. We just got back from the doctor's office."

"The doctor's office? Is everything okay?" Auntie Sue sounded concerned.

"No..." Emily tried to stay relaxed, as tears rolled down her face again.

"What's wrong? Are you crying? I'm coming over right now. Stay there!" Auntie Sue hung up before Emily had a chance to respond, and ten minutes later, she was at the door. Emily ran into her aunt's sturdy arms and sobbed for a few minutes. She looked down and pressed her finger against her lips to remind Auntie Sue to be quiet and led her aunt to the kitchen.

Auntie Sue was three inches taller than Ma. She had a stocky frame with broad shoulders, thick arms and her dyed black hair was tightly permed against her round face. She and Ma shared few common features, which led most people to believe they were just friends. Auntie Sue and her husband were retired and their two grown kids, Rachael and Rick, lived in Toronto. Emily seldom saw her cousins, although she and Rachael had been close at one time.

"Okay Emily, tell me what is wrong," Auntie Sue whispered.

Emily told her about their meeting with Dr. Eng. "He said it's liver cancer and she only had four weeks to live."

Auntie Sue mumbled in Chinese about Ma's bad luck, wiped her eyes and blew her nose.

"I'm sure if Ma had changed doctors, we would have found out about this earlier," Emily said slamming her fist on the table. "Look what happened to Dad!"

Auntie Sue nodded. "Ai, Emily, what can we do about it now?" She sighed. "I warned your mother about her constant worrying. I told her, "Ai-ya, if you keep thinking you are sick, you will be soon! Now look what has happened!" She continued to complain in Chinese about Ma's negative attitude after Dad died.

Emily said nothing while her aunt ranted. They sat in silence after Auntie Sue had finished, until she felt it was safe to speak. She looked at her aunt's tear-stained face and whispered, "What are we going to do?"

"Don't worry," Auntie Sue said as she reached across the table to hold Emily's hand. "We will take care of your mother. Do you think she understands what is going on?"

"I'm not sure. She knows she has cancer, but Dr. Eng didn't tell her how long or anything."

Auntie Sue nodded. "Let's not worry her anymore, Emily. She knows enough."

Emily nodded. She searched her aunt's face for reassurance. Auntie Sue opened her arms and gave Emily a hug.

"Don't worry," she said. "I will move in with your ma and make sure she is looked after."

A heaviness seemed to lift from Emily's shoulders, and she sighed out loud. "Will you? I would feel much better if you were around, Auntie Sue."

"It is no problem. She is my only sister, Emily." Auntie Sue wiped her eyes again, then got up and began to rummage through Ma's cupboards. She pulled a stockpot out and filled it with water. "I'm going to make some calls. There must be a good soup that I can brew to make your Ma stronger." She dialed several friends' numbers, jotting down ingredients as she spoke until she had a soup recipe. A few hours later, after her husband had dropped off the ingredients and clothes for Auntie Sue, a strong smelling, bitter concoction filled the house.

"What's that?" asked Ma as she appeared in the kitchen.

"I'm making you some soup," proclaimed Auntie Sue proudly.

"I'm not hungry," replied Ma.

"You don't need to be hungry. Just drink it!"

Ma jutted out her lower lip and crossed her arms over her chest.

"Ma, the doctor said you need to rest more and eat better. Auntie Sue is going to stay with you and take care of you." Emily touched Ma's hand. Ma opened her mouth as if to protest, but said nothing

At her aunt's urging, Emily left for home. Cars, signs, lights flashed past her, leading her to home. She drove down the driveway, uncertain of the time. Inside the apartment, she dropped her purse and bags to the ground, before continuing to the living room. The message light was flashing on her answering machine, but she walked past it and slumped into the couch. *What's going to happen? What am I going to do?* She closed her eyes and wiped away the tears again.

Emily was jerked out of her reverie by the phone in her living room. She had fallen asleep. Now she listened from her couch to the answering machine.

"Em, it's me. I'll be half an hour late – traffic. See you soon, Sweetie."

Emily stretched and looked at her watch: 4:45. *Oh God, Sam is coming. Where has the time gone?* Her heart pumped as she raced to the bathroom and looked at her face. Her eyeliner had washed off and her hair had lost its bounce. She turned the faucet on and began to freshen up. Emily had met Sam at a bar a year ago, where she had gone with her friend Jane. She applied some new makeup and brushed her shoulder-length straight hair. *Better.* She smiled as she picked up the volumizer, thinking how at the time she didn't care for the thin, dark-haired Caucasian guy, standing beside his tall blonde friend. They had brought drinks to their table and Emily found her attention monopolized by Sam; the blonde flirted with Jane. She sprayed her hair back to life. *Done.*

She turned and moved quickly into the bedroom. Her form-fitting black dress hung outside the closet door. It had a sweetheart neckline that flattered her slim figure. Emily had worn a similar, but more casual style of dress, on her first date with Sam. Sam had asked her out at the end of the evening at the bar, and she agreed just to be polite. Nothing came of the evening for Jane and the blonde, disappointing her friend.

She discovered on their first date that Sam had a good sense of humour, and Emily found herself laughing easily with him. In fact, she had such a fun time with him on the first date, she agreed to a second date. That led to more dates and before she knew it, they were couple. She wiggled into the black dress and pulled on a pair of nylons. Unaccustomed to walking in three-inch high black pumps, she grabbed the wall to brace herself when she lost her footing. *Goddammit!* She threw each shoe aside, cursing herself for her foolishness and took out an older pair of flatter shoes from her closet. She went to her dresser and put on the heart pendant necklace Sam had given her for their anniversary. He surprised her with it earlier, saying he "couldn't wait." She smiled. He was always so thoughtful.

Knock. Knock. "Hello," called a voice from the front door.

She rushed from the bedroom.

"Hello Sweetie," Sam said as he picked her up and gave her a kiss.

Emily locked onto his soft lips. After she released him, he handed her a large bouquet of flowers.

"Oh, they're beautiful!" she said as the scent of fragrant roses and orchids filled the room. She arranged the flowers in a wide glass vase and placed them in the dining room.

"You look beautiful, Em," Sam said as he stroked her arm. "Ready?"

Emily nodded. She put her feet into her old shoes, grabbed her purse, coat and locked the door.

The night air was cool and she shivered as they walked arm in arm towards Sam's car.

"You cold? Come on then." His arm at her waist pushed her forward, and she giggled as they raced to get into his car. "Warm now?"

She nodded as the heat from the car soothed her body and she relaxed. As they drove to the restaurant, Sam told her about his day at the office. He was an accountant and worked for a large firm in the city. Sam laughed out loud as he told her about something that happened with a client. *What did he say?* She tried to laugh, but only managed a few grunts. At a red light, he wrinkled up his forehead and studied her.

"Everything okay? How was your day?"

"Oh, fine. I've got a bit of a headache because I'm starving." She smiled, avoiding Sam's gaze as she stroked his hand. He squeezed hers and drove a little faster.

At the restaurant, Emily fiddled with a bread stick as she sipped her glass of red wine. She only had wine on special occasions and felt light-headed and weak from it.

"What do you feel like tonight? The usual?" Sam looked up from his menu at Emily.

"Too many choices," she replied. Sam nodded.

She looked at the menu and all the foods she loved on it: *Hearts of Romaine, Fresh Oysters, Hickory Smoked Salmon, Angus Beef Steak*. Her stomach grumbled, but she didn't feel hungry. During their first date here, Sam had talked for what felt like hours, and she enjoyed listening. She had laughed at his silly stories and giggled at his facial expressions. Although she seldom drank martinis, Sam had recommended one that tasted like punch, a Cosmo or something? She was on her second one. During dessert, Sam reached across the table and held her hand. He became quiet and they listened to the jazz band playing as they caressed each other's hands. Emily liked the smooth feel of Sam's hand and was feeling quite turned on, when something churned in her stomach. She bolted from the table into the bathroom. The sink was two feet ahead of her when she pushed the door open. Emily gagged to keep the vomit down until she was safely over the sink. Afterwards, she gargled with tap water and looked at the mess. Her bloodshot eyes and flushed face glared back from the mirror. *I'm disgusting.* She blotted the sweat from her forehead and steadied herself against the sink. When she finally felt like she could walk, she slowly made her way back to the table. Sam jumped up and helped her to her seat. *I'm an idiot!* she thought as she looked up to face Sam. She expected to be chided, maybe ridiculed, but instead was surprised to see compassion in his eyes. Her feelings for him grew.

Sam's voice brought her back to the present. "Em, you're so quiet. Are you okay?" Sam reached for her hand.

She tried to smile.

"Let's order first, okay?"

Sam nodded and they ordered.

After the waiter left, Emily took a breath. "It's my mother," she said.

"Yes?"

"Well, I went with her to see the family doctor and he told me she is dy..." Emily choked up and cursed herself for crying.

"What happened?"

She shrugged her shoulders. She didn't understand and struggled to tell Sam what she knew.

"I'm sorry. I didn't want to ruin our night." She fiddled with her napkin.

"It's okay, Em, this is your mother. Do you want to go home?" Sam looked worried.

"I don't know. Let's just finish dinner and go back to my place." Sam agreed. Emily tried to eat her food, but her stomach was in knots. She was relieved when they left and returned to her apartment.

Sam held Emily as they lay on the couch at her place. She felt cold and shivered.

"How can I help?" Sam kept asking. Emily didn't know. Sam had never met her mother and she had no intention of introducing him to her, unless she had to. She didn't respond to him, but held on tight.

Sam spent the night trying to comfort her, but still Emily couldn't sleep. Vivid images and memories of Ma from childhood flashed through her mind, disturbing her. She felt exhausted in the morning and stayed in bed. She sent Sam home.

The weekend seemed to be moving in slow motion. She called Ma to check up on her Saturday and Sunday. Ma was a bit suspicious by her second call.

"Why do you keep asking me if I all right?" Ma sounded annoyed.

"Dr. Eng told you to get more rest, remember?"

"I am resting more. Last night I was tired so we finished the Mahjong game early," Ma said.

"Early? How early?" *Is this a bad sign?*

"Nine o'clock. You okay?" Ma heard her concern.

"Yes, I'm okay. But what about you?" She heard her voice raise.

"I OKAY too!" Her mother insisted. "You sound like have cold. You have cold?"

How does she always change the conversation? She wanted to yell at her mother for not listening like she always did, but what was the point in upsetting her? Instead, she went along. "Well, maybe I'm catching a cold?" she fibbed.

"Oh. You want me to make soup?"

"A...sure," Emily responded uncertain. Ma went on for a few minutes about the importance of good soup. Emily followed the conversation, making up her symptoms until it concluded with the type of soup her mother was going to make.

Emily hung up the phone. What had she learned? *Nothing. Just lies as usual between them.* She paced around restlessly. Cancer. She didn't know what to make of it. No one in the family had had it. She went into her office and turned the computer on. She typed liver cancer and began to read all the articles generated by her search. Emily's face reddened when she read Hepatitis B carriers were at risk for developing this cancer. Ma had been a carrier all her life. What the hell had that stupid Dr. Eng been doing? "I hate that man," she screamed and cussed. She raced through the articles as images of Dr. Eng's toothless smile flashed through her mind. She wanted to find something, anything that would prove Dr. Eng was wrong, that her mother could be helped. Most of the research she found had been done in Japan, but it gave her a list of treatment options. She printed out several articles to discuss with the specialist.

Monday morning's bright sun shone through the vertical blinds in Emily's room and she rolled over to hide her face in the pillow. Her pajamas were soaked from sweat and she stuck her leg out from her blankets to cool off. Emily rubbed her eyes and wondered if she had slept. All night, she thought about how incompetent Dr. Eng was and why he hadn't done more to prevent this. She picked up her watch and saw that it was eight o'clock. Pushing the blankets off herself, she pulled herself out of bed, into the bathroom and turned on the shower. Emily went through her usual routine and got dressed. She put an extra scoop of coffee into the machine and forced herself to eat some cereal. She wanted to feel strong. At nine o'clock she got into the car and drove to her mother's place.

"Hi Ma," she called out as she entered the house and made her way into the kitchen. Ma was sitting down at the kitchen table, holding half a piece of toast. Auntie Sue had gone to her house to do some housework and would return by lunch.

"I made soup for you. It's in the fridge – you want it now?"

"No it's okay, I'll take it home with me. You okay?" Emily studied Ma's face. Her skin looked smooth, although a few wrinkles and dark circles could be seen around her eyes.

"Sure." Ma nodded as she chewed on her toast and drank her tea. "Not very hungry – old people don't need so much." Ma put the toast down and yawned. "Time to go?"

Emily nodded. She felt prepared to meet this cancer specialist.

She drove to the medical building where Dr. Fung's office was. It was a new structure of glass and steel. They took the elevator up to the office and waited. No other patients were in the waiting room, and Emily flipped through a magazine quickly as she watched for the doctor to enter the room. Dr. Fung turned out to be an older gentleman, around Dr. Eng's age. He was dressed in a white lab coat. Emily and Ma followed him into the examination room.

"I'm Dr. Fung," he said speaking in English, as he extended his hand out to shake Ma's and Emily's hand.

"Please have a seat."

Emily and Ma sat down across from Dr. Fung.

"Hmm...I've looked at Dr. Eng's notes, and I also had a chance to see your CT scan, Mrs. Chow. This is what we see." Dr. Fung pointed to the image of Ma's liver and where the tumor was. Ma looked confused.

Emily translated, as she had done all her childhood. She didn't know the word for CT scan, so she improvised with x-ray. Ma nodded.

"Okay," Dr. Fung said, "now, let's take a look." He got up and led them to the examination table. "Can you help her to get undressed?"

Emily nodded and assisted Ma with her clothing. Ma lay stiffly on the examination table.

"It's okay, Mrs. Chow," Dr. Fung tried to reassure her. His hands moved along the right side of Ma's abdomen. "Here," he said as he took Emily's hand. "This is the tumor. Quite large."

Emily ran her hand along a sausage that bulged from Ma's abdomen. It felt hard. She shivered.

Dr. Fung moved Ma's hand to touch her tumor, but she refused and shook her head silently. After the examination, Ma got dressed and they took their seats in front of Dr. Fung's desk again.

"What can we do?" Emily asked.

"I'm afraid it is too advanced to do anything."

She turned to look at Ma. Ma stared at the wall behind Dr. Fung's desk. A stoic expression was on her face. "What about surgery, liver transplantation or percutaneous ethanol injection?" Emily asked as she turned her attention back to Dr. Fung and showed him the list of treatment options and articles she found on the internet. Dr. Fung nodded quietly as she cited the statistics of success from these treatments.

"Some of these options might have been possible if we had caught it sooner. It's too late now for transplantation and some of the other experimental treatments you mentioned aren't even being done here, I'm afraid." Dr. Fung looked down.

"Too late...what do you mean?" Emily felt her heart racing.

"Emily, your mother has maybe four weeks to live. I'm afraid all we can do is make her comfortable. I'm sorry." Dr. Fung looked at Ma, who continued to stare silently at the wall.

Four weeks! Four weeks – how can this be? "Are you sure?" she finally asked feeling defeated.

"I'm afraid so," he replied.

Chapter Three

Emily walked into the kitchen and opened the fridge. It was dinner time: 5:30. She stared at the leftovers, poured herself a glass of orange juice and closed the fridge. She slowly moved back to the living room and slumped down onto the couch. She resumed staring at the television screen as she had all afternoon since her return home.

In the car, she couldn't stand the silence and her mother's sulking face. She whipped down the streets quickly, her mind searching for words of comfort. *What can I say?* At the doorway, she finally managed "get some rest" and left her mother to her aunt's care. *Thank God for Auntie Sue.* She was so relieved to be rid of her mother, but guilt overwhelmed her on the drive home. *I should do more!* More what?

News was on. Tears flooded her eyes several times as she watched: once during a commercial about drunk drivers, and how drinking can take a life; then during the news, when it was reported that a famous actor had died from a heart attack. She rubbed her chest, but still it ached.

The phone rang as she watched, but she didn't bother to answer it.

"Emily, it's me," she heard Sam say. "Are you there? Call me when you get home. Better yet, I'm coming over with some take-out. I'll see you soon."

Emily glanced at the red flashing light from her answering machine and sat back. She continued to flip through the channels. An hour later, there was a knock at the door.

Emily had given Sam a key to her apartment months ago. "Come in," she yelled over the noise of the television.

Sam opened the door. He stumbled over her things and came into the living room.

"Em?" Sam said as he turned the light on. "You're sitting in the dark. Are you okay?"

"Oh," she replied as she switched the television off and blinked several times to adjust to the lighted room. "I guess I'm okay."

Sam put the take-out food on the dining room table and walked over to her. Without looking, she knew it was Chinese food again. Sam seemed more Asian than she was at times.

"What happened?" he asked kneeling by her side.

"Nothing. Nothing good. The specialist said we are too late. The cancer is too advanced, and we can't do anything." Emily spoke flatly, as she wiped the tears from her face.

"I'm sorry, Emily." Sam tried to embrace her.

"Yeah, that stupid Dr. Eng. It's his fault! He's useless!" She pushed Sam aside and got up.

Sam moved out of her way and followed silently behind.

Emily began to open the Chinese take-out.

"Here, let me," said Sam, as he gently pushed her down into a chair. The smell of greasy noodles filled the air making her feel nauseous. Sam took some plates out and sat down. "Em, please, eat something," he urged.

She split the cheap wooden chopsticks that came with the food into two and picked up a small amount of noodles from the aluminum container. She pushed them around her plate. Sam dumped some Chinese broccoli and an egg roll on the plate.

"Enough, thanks," she said as she put her hand up.

Sam filled his plate and started to eat. He used his chopsticks like an expert, even though he claimed he'd only learned how to use them during university. He caught her watching and she responded by picking up some food.

"Thanks for bringing dinner," she said and gave his arm a squeeze. He was always so nice to her. When her car broke down three months ago, he went out of his way to drive her to work. Every morning he smiled as he fought traffic to get her to her office in Downsview. His office was the opposite direction, downtown. She thought for sure by the third day that he would tell her to take the subway, but he didn't. She did feel bad for him, but selfishly enjoyed it.

"Can you tell me some more about your meeting?" he asked gently.

Robotically, she took him step by step through the meeting with Dr. Fung.

"These treatments you suggested, is there anyone doing any of it here in the city?"

Her eyes widened. "I don't know. Do you think our hospitals do the treatments? Maybe I could get Ma into treatment here?" she asked quickly.

"I'm not sure," shrugged Sam. "But if you want to try, I'd be happy to help you call the hospitals."

"Oh, Sam, that would help me a lot," she said with some excitement. She moved the chopsticks to her mouth for the first time and was surprised to find she was hungry. Emily finished her plate and a second helping before grabbing the phone book. She wrote down all the hospital phone numbers on a piece of paper and showed it to Sam.

"Well," he said looking at the list, "it's probably too late in the evening to call. Most of the offices would be closed, don't you think?"

Emily saw that it was 7:30 and she nodded.

"The other thing I could do is speak with my cousin. Have you met Arnold?"

"Maybe once."

"He's a family doctor. Perhaps he could help us with names or speak with some specialists for us," Sam suggested.

"You think he would?"

"Sure. He's a nice guy, and we are first cousins," said Sam.

"That's a great idea," she said smiling.

"Okay, let me call him now." Sam picked up his cell and dialed.

Emily began to clear the table so Sam could take notes. She put the leftover food into the fridge. Arnold was not home, but Sam spoke with his wife and left an urgent message. She took out the articles she had gathered from the internet to show Sam. Liver cancer was a bigger problem in the Asian population, so most of the experimental treatments had been done abroad. She and Sam summarized the results of all the articles onto one page.

"Dr. Fung looked like he had heard of these treatments, so something must be happening here too, right?" She hoped.

"I don't know, Em," Sam said as he touched her hand. "We're going to find out, okay?" *Practical.* She loved him for his factual approach to things, but at this moment she felt defeated, like he wanted to crush her dreams. Feeling sullen, she moved to the couch to watch some television. Sam joined her, but she ignored him. She didn't want to be mean, but she couldn't help herself. *Why am I acting this way?* She looked at his elegantly shaped nose, wavy brown hair and square jawline. *So handsome. So White. So different from me.* She snapped back to the television with an uneasy feeling of repulsion. She didn't know why she had these feelings and tried to shake them off.

Arnold called back at nine o'clock. Emily listened as Sam explained the situation and the diagnosis. She got up and quietly started to tidy up the living room, glancing at Sam's face every now and then. *What is he saying?* She wondered as she shifted things around. After about ten minutes he hung up.

"Well?" she asked anxiously.

"He said he'd be happy to make some calls for us tomorrow."

"Really? That's wonderful!" She jumped up and grabbed Sam's hands. Then she asked slowly, "Does he think there is any hope?"

"He doesn't know, Emily," Sam said. "But we can at least try, right?"

Emily nodded.

Chapter Four

The next day, Emily woke up feeling almost refreshed. She had slept soundly, but upon waking realized she had dreamed about a figure she hadn't thought about in a while. Her old employer, Dr. Eric Lee, an acupuncturist, Chinese herbal medicine specialist and Chi Kung expert, had entered her dreams. She had taken a job working for Dr. Lee after graduating in April 1989. She had accepted a job offer at a rehabilitation firm, but it didn't start until September. For five months, she had toiled under Dr. Lee's rule. He was a demanding employer and expected her to assist him with treatment, as well as prepare herbal packages for patients. Emily enjoyed assisting the patients, but found she had horrible allergies to most of the Chinese herbs. Day in, day out, she sneezed and sniffled as she prepared the packages, with Dr. Lee offering little in assistance. Linda, the other assistant in the office, suggested she ask Dr. Lee to treat her allergies, after all, he was a self-proclaimed healer. Dr. Lee did treat her a couple of times, but her nose still ran and she left congested every day. She remained uncertain of Dr. Lee's powers, although patients she befriended from his clinic assured her of them. "He is a very powerful healer," some said. She knew he had helped some of his patients with migraine headaches, chronic fatigue and had even improved conditions like Lupus and Muscular Dystrophy. She also saw disgruntled patients leave the practice complaining of his high cost and ineffectiveness.

"They musta come early," Dr. Lee stressed in his poor English, when patients came in to see him.

"Early, we have chance. Late can do something, but more difficult."

Emily recalled this information as she showered. She wasn't sure how successful Dr. Lee had been with cancer, although he had been treating an older patient with bone cancer when she worked there. She got herself ready for the day and looked at her work calendar as she ate some cereal. *Maybe I should ask his opinion now?* Seeing she only had one report to finish, she decided she could see Dr. Lee that morning and work on her report in the afternoon. She finished her coffee and cleaned up before leaving.

In the car, she found the route to Dr. Lee's office easily. She parked in a nearby neighbourhood to avoid paying for street parking. It was 10:30. A good time to visit, she thought, since the office opened at 9:00 and usually quieted down around this time.

When she entered the office, only one patient was seated in the waiting area. She took a seat on the tired-looking furniture. Dr. Lee had added more chairs to his waiting area, she noticed, although the furniture still looked old. The familiar smell of moxibustion, an herbal stick that she lit and applied to the acupuncture points after the needles were removed, filled the air. The smell reminded her of pot.

Dr. Lee walked into the waiting room, wearing his usual white lab coat. It had been almost eight years since she had seen him. Still, he stood erect at six feet, had jet-black hair and his brown eyes twinkled. *Who would think he was* 65? He smiled at her and she stood up, but he motioned to the other woman to come into his office.

"Justa minute," he said to her and turned to follow his patient into his office.

Emily sat back down. She could see him taking the woman's pulses from her seat. Dr. Lee seemed to be listening as he pressed three fingers along the woman's arm to do a pulse diagnosis. He did this on both wrists, making little squiggly lines. He used this information to tell you what was weak in the body like the liver, kidney, spleen or heart. After an acupuncture treatment, he would show you how these bodily functions had improved. Then he'd send you home with some herbs to brew; more medicine to fix your condition. Emily looked at her watch. It was almost 11:00 now. *Do I really have time for this?* She got up and walked to the receptionist's area, but it was empty. Through the clear glass, she saw the phone she had used and the little desk she had shared with Linda. Why was there no one working there now?

Desperate. That's what Linda had said about the patients who came to see Dr. Lee. "He's their last hope when no one else can help." They had whispered quietly over lunch on the small desk about the different patients and their predicaments. *Am I desperate too?* She turned away and stood back in front of her seat, uncertain of whether she should sit or not. Suddenly the office door flew open and she jumped, startled by it.

"Emily, comma in," said Dr. Lee as he stood in the doorway.

Emily's heart pumped as she followed Dr. Lee into his office. She took a seat and waited for him to close the office door and walk around to his desk.

"Long time," he said smiling. "Are you married now?"

"No," she replied. "Where's the assistant?"

"My wife is coming after lunch. She will answer the phones."

"Oh yes, I heard you got married about five years ago." she said.

Dr. Lee nodded and took a picture of his son from his desk. "My son," he said proudly.

"Very nice," she said as she relaxed in her seat studying the picture of the smiling boy in a sailor's suit. "How old now?"

"Almost four. You should get married early, not like me," he urged.

Emily nodded and gave the picture back to him. "One day, when it's right. Is your wife also a doctor?"

Dr. Lee nodded and explained his wife had been working full time as an acupuncturist in China, but now only had afternoons to assist him at the office since she was busy at home. A babysitter watched their son in the afternoon.

"Your English has improved," she said complimenting him. He smiled broadly, and they continued to talk about Dr. Lee's home and work life for another ten minutes or so.

"Very busy," Dr. Lee said of his practice. "Today, you come at a good time." He sat back in his chair and waited for Emily to speak.

She took a breath and began, "My mother has liver cancer."

"Oh, very serious," Dr. Lee said shaking his head. "Tell me more," he said and picked up his pen.

Emily relayed what the specialist had told her. "Can you do anything for her?"

"Of course!" he responded. "Always can do my best. Can make her stronger to fight!" He clenched his hand into a fist. "But need to start treatment very soon," he urged. "Faster come in, better can help."

She nodded. "I am looking into some hospital treatments too."

"Sure. Maybe can do both, Western medicine and Chinese medicine together, but don't wait too long to start Chinese medicine."

"Okay. I will get back to you by the middle of the week." Emily stood up.

Dr. Lee extended his hand to her. She shook it.

"Don't a worry, Emily. Can help your mother," he said with assurance.

Emily looked at Dr. Lee's confident smile and nodded. She left the office quickly as she could see that it was already 12 noon.

Chapter Five

When Emily returned home, she had a quick lunch and booted up her computer. She got her notes ready and began writing. She worked steadily, not thinking about the time until the phone rang.

"Hello?"

"Em, it's me," said Sam.

"Hi Sam. What's up?"

"I just wanted to let you know that Arnold called and said he's put in a few calls for us and is waiting to hear back from some people."

"Really? That's great news!" she said excitedly. "I did some research too and went to see my old employer Dr. Lee."

"Oh?"

"Yes, Dr. Lee is an acupuncturist, traditional Chinese medicine doctor and a Chi Kung specialist."

"Okay..." said Sam uncertain.

"I'll explain it to you later, but anyways he said he can treat Ma!"

"Oh. Guess that is good?"

"Of course it is!" she said hotly. *Why would he say that?* "Are you coming over later?"

"Sure," said Sam.

"I'll tell you all about Dr. Lee then. He's treated lots of very sick people and with lots of success," she said and hung up the phone.

After she hung up, she wondered about Sam's reaction to Dr. Lee. *Why wasn't he as fired up about Dr. Lee as she was?* Chinese medicine has been around for hundreds of years, right? she thought. She actually knew very little about Chinese medicine; all she had known were the experiences of patients that Dr. Lee treated. *Isn't that enough?* She didn't want to be distracted by doubts, so she turned to her work. Focused, she soon completed the reports she wanted done. Satisfied, she turned her computer off and went into the kitchen to prepare dinner. It was five o'clock. Sam got off work at five, so he would be over by six at the latest.

Emily placed a large pot of water on the stove for the spaghetti and made a quick pasta sauce with canned tomatoes and spices. She opened a bag of salad, put it into a wooden salad bowl and added her last red pepper and tomato to it. She took her strainer out to drain her pasta when she heard a knock on the door.

"Come in, Sam," she called out in the direction of the door.

Sam let himself in and came into the kitchen.

"Can I help?" he asked.

"Do you want to set the table?"

"Sure." Sam took some plates and cutlery out of the cupboards and went over to the dining room.

Emily brought the food over, then took a leftover opened wine bottle from the fridge and sat down. "I hope you don't mind this opened bottle," she said as she uncorked and poured some wine into their glasses.

"Fine by me," said Sam smiling as he sat down.

"Okay, let's eat."

"Good pasta," Sam said after his first mouthful. "Okay, tell me about this Dr. Lee."

"Thanks. Sure. I worked for Dr. Lee about eight years ago when I graduated from school," she said as she ate.

"Umhum."

"Do you know anything about Chinese medicine?"

"Not really."

"Well, he's trained in China in three specialties: acupuncture, traditional Chinese medicine and Chi Kung."

"Yeah?" Sam helped himself to a second serving of pasta and offered to serve Emily more.

"No thanks, I'm going to have some salad when I'm done," she said as she finished her plate. "Anyways, you know that acupuncture involves treating people with needles; Chinese medicine uses herbs to treat ailments and, well, Chi Kung has to do with healing with your life energy."

"What does that mean?" Sam asked.

"You know, your Chi, or life energy."

"Okay..." said Sam.

"Look, to be honest, I've never studied it formally, but what I understand is that Dr. Lee is able to use life energy to treat patient aliments or something like that."

"Okay..." Sam sounded skeptical.

"I know, it sounds kinda weird, but people said it worked," she said loudly, determined to hide the uncertainty she felt.

"Like how? And what did he treat?"

"Well, when I worked there, he treated different chronic conditions like fatigue, headaches, Lupus, Muscular Dystrophy and this one guy had one side of his face paralyzed that Dr. Lee was able to cure."

"Really? Do the results last?"

"Seemed like it, although people had to come back sometimes for a refresher."

"Hmm..."

She hoped Sam was satisfied with her answers, although she wasn't even sure she was. *Why was he asking so many questions? Isn't he supposed to be supporting me?* She could feel resentment building. "What about you?" she asked to change the subject. "Did you hear back from your cousin?"

"Yeah, I'm afraid so." Sam put his fork down.

"What?"

"Well, he said he spoke to one of the specialists at Princess Margaret Hospital, and apparently no one is doing any of the treatments you found in your research."

"Oh," Emily said deflated.

"But, he said that the specialist is aware of a drug trial that will be running at Sunnybrook Hospital in a couple of months."

"A couple of months? That might be too late!" She pounded her fist on the table.

"I know, I know," said Sam. "The other option is to have your mother get treatment with the specialist Arnold knows."

"Really? This person would be willing to see Ma?"

"That's what Arnold said. They can always try conventional methods like chemotherapy on her."

Emily sighed. "Would it help her?"

"I think so, but I'm not sure," Sam said as he took her hands. "You have to get your mom's family doctor to make the referral."

"God!" exclaimed Emily. "That may be difficult."

"Why?"

"Oh, you don't know Dr. Eng. He thinks he knows everything. He'll never agree to make a referral for Ma!" Emily stood up and pushed her chair into the table.

"It's up to you, Em." Sam said softly as he came over to her side. "Don't you think it's worth a try?"

"I guess so," she said slowly. "What do you think about Dr. Lee?"

"Honestly, I don't know. I don't have any experience in this area, but this energy thing sounds weird, I mean, how can you cure anybody this way?"

Emily pushed Sam away and turned her back to him. *How can he say that?* She regretted asking this "goi-law" for his opinion. She wiped the tears from her eyes and tried to speak with a clear voice, almost making a proclamation. "I don't know how it works; I just know that it sometimes does!"

Sam nodded and turned her to face him. "Okay, I know you're not sure. Why don't you just call Dr. Eng and talk to him about this?"

Emily sighed again. "Guess so."

Sam embraced her.

Emily dug her face into his neck and clung on tight. *How can this be happening?* Wetness from her eyes soaked Sam's shirt collar, but Sam held on. She felt so confused. Dr. Lee said he could help Ma. Dr. Eng said just make her comfortable. Now Sam's cousin is suggesting referral to another specialist. She wanted to hit something! She pushed Sam down and kissed him hard, almost pinning him to the floor. Her body took over, and she gladly forgot her worries.

After Sam left in the morning, Emily went to do her assessment. She usually enjoyed assessing people for jobs, but today found it a strain to smile and make small talk. She followed her forms, robotically instructing the client through the various tests and exercises. By noon, the client had completed the tasks, and she thankfully packed her briefcase.

"Hey Emily, how's it going?" asked Dan the physiotherapist, as he walked into the office.

"Oh, fine," she said looking up from her desk.

"How was your client today?"

"He was good – seems like a good candidate."

"Good," he said, adding. "Everything okay?"

"Just tired, why?" she said wondering if she was acting odd.

"No reason. You don't seem like your usual self today, that's all." Dan looked concerned.

"Oh." Emily bit her lip to hold back the tears welling in her eyes. "Look, I've gotta go. Can we talk later?"

"Sure. Hey, I didn't mean to upset you," Dan said as Emily rushed out the door.

Safely inside her car, Emily checked her face in the vanity mirror. She had managed to hide the tears from Dan and now fixed her makeup. After she used up her energy on Sam last night, she called her mother. Ma sounded so empty, she recalled as she started up the car and proceeded out the parking lot.

"How was your day, Ma?" she had asked. She was calling her daily; something she used to dread doing.

"Okay."

"What did you do?"

"Auntie Sue want to play Mahjong, but I don't feel like." Ma spoke flatly.

"What? Mahjong is your favourite game! Why didn't you play?"

"Ai, I getting old Emily. I told Auntie Sue to play, and I stay home to rest and watch television."

"So what did you do?"

"Auntie Sue decide not to play, and she take me out to the mall for a walk."

"Did you enjoy your walk?" she asked hopefully.

"I got tired after only ten minutes of walking! Then we sat down to rest, before I walk again. We left after half an hour."

When she spoke with her aunt, she confirmed that Ma seemed to be more fatigued than usual. She was worried.

"Don't worry," Auntie Sue said. "I'm making some more soup for her, and I rented some Chinese movies that will make her laugh."

She tried to take solace in her aunt's words.

Emily parked her car and walked up to her apartment. She had picked up a hamburger and fries on her way home and placed the unopened bag on the table. As she poured herself some juice, she noticed how empty her refrigerator was. She sighed and sat down to eat. It was

1:30. *I wonder if this is a good time to call Dr. Eng?* She hated calling *that man,* but finally did agree with Sam that it was worth a try. As she chewed her junk food, she rehearsed what she would say to Dr. Eng and what words would stroke his ego. When she felt ready, she put her half-eaten hamburger down, picked up the phone and dialed.

"Dr.'s Eng's office." The secretary answered.

"Hi, it's Emily Chow. Can I speak with Dr. Eng?"

"What is this about, Emily?"

"It's about my mother, Yu Lin Chow."

"I'll see if he is available. Hold please."

Emily waited and listened to the on hold music on the phone.

"Hello, Emily?" It was Dr. Eng.

"Hi, Dr. Eng," she said brightly.

"I'm glad you called. I was wondering if you could speak to your mother for me."

"Sure. About what?"

"Dr. Fung wants to do a biopsy on the tumor next Monday to confirm it is cancer, so your mother needs to go in for some blood work. She can go to the lab anytime."

"A biopsy? Is that still necessary? I thought everyone said it is cancer." Emily was confused.

"Yes, it is cancer. This is just a technical procedure to confirm what we already know."

"Okay, I can speak with her, but I was calling you for another reason."

"Oh?"

"Yes, I want your opinion about something."

"Yes?" Dr. Eng sounded eager.

"What do you think about some of the work being done in cancer in Toronto? Do you think it might be worthwhile for my mother to see someone in the city?" She chose her words carefully, hoping it would please Dr. Eng.

"Hmm," Dr. Eng said slowly. "You know there are some good specialists in Toronto, but in your mother's case I'm not sure if it is worth their time to see her. Really, what we need to do is just make her comfortable. Do you want her to suffer more by engaging in treatment that won't help?"

"How do you know it won't help? Don't you think we should at least try?" Emily sounded desperate.

"Ai, Emily. I know this is hard for you to hear. I'm sorry, but really, there is nothing we can do for her."

"Let me try, Dr. Eng. Write me a referral, there's a Dr. Smith that was recommended to me. Just write a little note for me and I'll take care of the rest," she pleaded.

"Yes, I know that specialist. He is good, but in your mother's case it would just be wasting his time."

"How can you be sure?" She tried to control the anger in her voice.

"Emily, please. Just take your mother in for the blood work and the biopsy is next Monday, okay? I've got to go now." Dr. Eng hung up.

Emily stared at her phone and slammed it down. "Damn that man!" She cursed loudly as she paced her apartment, stopping only to wipe the tears that flowed down her face. After twenty minutes, she sat down exhausted. *What choices did she have now?*

In the afternoon, Emily found herself driving to Oakville. She had tried to work on a report, but was distracted by thoughts about Dr. Lee and Dr. Eng. She managed to get some information down before deciding she had done enough to piece it together later. Exiting the highway, she started to follow the usual route home, but turned the opposite direction towards the cemetery. She drove past the rows and rows of neatly lined headstones: gray, brown and white structures, semicircular or square shaped. Yellowing grass was changing to green and she wound the car past the administration building to the section of the cemetery where gravestones were laid flat on the earth. *To conserve space.* She parked and stared at the sea of green and yellow before her. *Is this the right section?* Holding the flowers she had picked up from the corner store, she walked gingerly through the grass, almost jumping when she realized she was on a gravesite, eyes darting fast, searching for the right stone. Relieved at last, she bent over to brush off the dirt from her father's gray granite gravestone and pulled out the grass that threatened to cover his name:

Chow Gin Yu

September 15, 1930 – December 10, 1995

The rest of the inscription was written in Chinese. She could not read it, but Ma said it paid honour to Dad and was important to put on. Emily traced her finger along the Chinese characters, enjoying the feel of the cool granite. An empty plastic vase was at the head of the gravestone and she took it to fill with water at a nearby hose. When she returned, she pushed the vase back into the ground and placed the yellow tulips she bought into it. The quietness of this sanctuary soothed her, and she breathed in fully as she looked around. A voice caught her attention, and she turned to see an elderly gentleman tending a gravesite two rows over to her right. He seemed to be speaking quietly and placed some beautiful red roses into a plastic vase. She looked around. Most of the burial sites looked well-groomed with fresh and planted flowers, trees and bushes. Emily and Ma had planted a dwarf tree and some of Ma's favourite flowers in the first spring after his death. Last fall, Emily planted tulip bulbs and was happy to see their pink and orange blossoms opened to the bright sun.

"Hi, Dad," she said as she stroked the stone.

"Do you like the flowers? I miss you..." She stopped and looked away, blinking fast. What would Dad say? How was she supposed to help Ma? She sighed. Dad wouldn't know what to do. He'd probably depend on good ole Dr. Eng. After all, he was like "family to us." Emily yanked out some grass and threw it in the air.

Dad had run a restaurant in downtown Oakville. It was a small place with six booths, six tables and a long front counter with stools that served Canadian and Chinese foods. Dad did all the cooking and baking. Emily loved the lemon cream pie he made, and he used to bring leftover filling from the pies home. He loved to spoil her. When Emily was old enough to go to school, Ma started to work at the restaurant during the day. Emily tried to hide the fact her dad owned The Rotunda Restaurant. It always worsened the taunts at school with kids giving her "chop suey chops" or insinuating the food was made with domestic animals. "Chinamen use cat meat in their food!" She never ate any of this so-called Chinese food at home. As far as she knew, it was all made up food for the Canadian public. Oddly enough, her dad's restaurant was wildly popular, and she saw a few too many of her high school friends dining there. When Dr. Eng dropped in, as he often would, Emily's dad always came out of the kitchen to greet him, and, of course, give him his dinner for free. Emily recalled how her dad had bragged about Dr. Eng's visits, and how proud he was to be able to give the man free food, like it was a privilege or something. *Like that man deserved it.* She got up and stretched. The hard ground was making her back sore.

"Bye, Dad," she said and blew a kiss as she walked back to her car. It was five o'clock and she felt a bit hungry. She drove through rush hour traffic to Ma's place.

"Hello?" she called out as she let herself in.

"Emily?" Ma called as she came out of the kitchen. "What you doing here? No work today?"

"I finished work early and went to visit Dad. There's too much traffic to drive home, so I thought I'd visit for a while."

Ma smiled. Auntie Sue emerged from the kitchen with Ma's apron on.

"Stay for dinner!" She insisted. "I am making some very good fish. Fresh."

Emily nodded and the three women moved into the kitchen.

"Can I help?" she offered.

Auntie Sue shook her head and place some cut oranges in front of Emily and Ma. "Everything is okay. Eat and relax with your Ma."

Emily sucked on an orange slice and looked at her mother. The dark circles under her eyes seemed to have faded and she chewed on the orange with interest.

"You feeling better?" she asked.

"More hungry," Ma said. "Your auntie's cooking too good. Make me hungry."

Auntie Sue laughed out loud and complimented Ma on her cooking. The two women argued for a few minutes in Chinese about who was the better cook. Emily smiled. Her mother always seemed happy with Auntie Sue. Well, they did argue, but they made up and laughed, unlike when she argued with her mother.

After a delicious dinner of steamed pickerel, boiled chicken and Chinese greens, Emily forced Auntie Sue out of the kitchen so she could clean up. Ma and Auntie Sue moved into the family room and started to watch a Chinese video. It must have been a comedy because Emily could hear Auntie Sue laugh loudly; Ma was chuckling as well. She finished the dishes and went over to the living room. She stopped at the doorway like an observer, watching the two women laughing as they sat on the couch.

"Sit down," Auntie Sue said as she motioned with her hand to a spot between them.

"No, no," she said, "I'll sit here." She sat in the armchair adjacent to them. It was getting late.

"Emily, you don't understand show, right?" Ma asked.

She shrugged her shoulders. "Some," she said. "But it's okay, I have to leave soon."

Auntie Sue paused the video. "Do you want to watch something else before you go?"

She shook her head. "Maybe we can talk a bit?"

Auntie Sue shut the television off and both women turned their attention to her.

"I spoke with Dr. Eng the other day."

"Yes?" Ma sounded nervous.

"He wants you to go to Dr. Fung's office for some blood work and then Dr. Fung wants to do something called a biopsy."

Ma looked confused.

"I can take your Ma tomorrow for the blood work," Auntie Sue offered. "When is the biopsy?"

"I think they want to do it early next week."

"More blood!" Ma retorted. "It's not good to take so much blood!"

"Yes, I agree. Your Ma has told me about all the tests and blood she has had taken out of her. Not good for the health." Auntie Sue shook her head.

"I'm sorry, Ma," Emily began, "I was also wondering if you might like to see a Chinese doctor in Toronto. I don't know if you remember me mentioning working for him when I graduated. He does acupuncture, gives herbs and this other thing. I talked to him about you and he said he can help." Emily realized she didn't know how to explain Chi Kung to them. *Let Dr. Lee tell them about it.*

"Chinese doctor would be good," Auntie Sue said as she turned to Ma who was nodding. "They know more about our bodies. When can we go? I can take your Ma anytime."

"I have to make an appointment. Would Friday or Saturday work? I am free one of those days," Emily said relieved but pleased with their reaction.

"Sure. You let us know." Auntie Sue continued to talk to Ma in Chinese about the benefits of a Chinese trained doctor.

"Okay," Emily said as she stood up. "I'd better go. Thank you for dinner," and she walked over to give her Auntie Sue a peck on the cheek like she normally did. Her mother didn't move as Emily stood up and backed away from the two women. It was always easy to hug Auntie Sue. Auntie Sue was affectionate to everyone, even to Ma. She tried to remember the last time her mother showed her any affection and all she could think of was holding Ma's hand when she was four or five years old. *Shouldn't I give Ma a kiss?* Undecided, she waved at the doorway and her mother smiled at her like nothing was wrong. She turned and walked to the front door. Ma and Auntie Sue were discussing Chinese medicine and who had good experiences with it or bad experiences with it. *They seemed so close, unlike us.* She sighed and unlocked the door.

At the door, she started to leave, but Auntie Sue stopped her. She whispered, "Your Ma seems to be doing better. Eating more, but still seems a bit weak. Chinese medicine is good idea." She smiled at Emily.

Emily nodded, almost proud of herself. Her aunt gave her a hug and she left for home.

Chapter Six

In the morning, she finished writing a report and started another one before getting ready for her afternoon appointment. She had spoken with Dr. Lee when his office opened and let her aunt know that their appointment was on Saturday at 10 am. Since Auntie Sue didn't know Toronto that well, Emily offered to pick them up. Instead her aunt suggested they drive to Emily's place first and then they could all go together. Emily felt relieved that she didn't have to do the extra driving.

She attended her one o'clock work appointment. "Hi, I'm Emily Chow," she said as she shook the waiting client's hand. "Today, I am going to put you through a variety of tests to assess your suitability for the job that you applied for. This way, please." After the man signed the medical release form, she led him to the testing equipment. They worked steadily through the day.

"Okay, sir," she said to her client. "We're all done." It was 4:30 pm.

"Hey, Emily," Dan called out. "All done for the day?"

"Yep," she said with a smile.

"I'm glad to see you're feeling better," he said with a grin.

"Thanks," she said with a wave. *I haven't thought about Ma all day!* she thought as she walked to her car. She sat down and touched the steering wheel. *Ma's okay. She's doing better.* She assured herself before starting up the engine and positioning the car in rush hour traffic. Sam was coming over after work for an early movie and dinner. Emily wasn't sure if she was up to going out and drove slowly home. Once in her apartment, she slumped down on the couch. She had just picked up the remote when she heard a knock, followed by the sound of the key unlocking the door.

"Hello?" Sam called as he walked in.

"In here" she said from the couch.

"You okay?"

She nodded. "Just tired."

"Come on." Sam offered his hand and he pulled her off the couch. "I think a movie is just what you need to get your mind off of things."

"Think so?"

He nodded and began to pull her forward. "Come on sleepy one!"

She laughed and let herself go into Sam's arms. "Hmm," she said as held him and pecked his lips. Sam's warm tongue reached for hers and they remained entangled for a longer taste. She exhaled. "I think I feel better now," she said smiling.

"That's good," Sam said and he kissed her one more time.

Outside, night had yet to descend. They walked slowly arm and arm down the street to the local movie theatre. Pockets of people gathered around the entrance, and Sam led Emily through the crowd to the ticket booth. "Two," he said as he pulled out his wallet. Inside, they bought popcorn and a drink to tie them over before dinner. Emily munched on the popcorn and looked around happily. It wasn't too busy for a Wednesday night. The lights dimmed and Sam reached over to hold her hand. She leaned back into her seat and put her right foot up against the empty chair in front of her and watched.

Two and a half hours later, they left the theatre and decided to have Italian food at the restaurant across the street. She laughed as they jaywalked across the street.

"I haven't seen you like this in a while, Em," Sam said smiling as he opened the restaurant door.

She nodded as she realized she had not thought about Ma again. She looked down feeling guilty as she followed Sam to their table,

"Hey, this is a good thing that you relax," Sam insisted. "You can't help if you are stressed out all the time, right?"

"Yeah, you're probably right." She nodded her head and assured herself. *Ma's doing fine.* Her eyes narrowed as she looked at Sam.

"You saw your mother yesterday, right?" he asked.

"Yes."

"And?"

"And she is doing okay, and Auntie Sue is with her."

"There you go," said Sam with determination. He studied the menu then put it down after a few minutes. "Okay, I'm ready. Are you?"

Emily looked at the entrée choices: pasta, pizza and meat. Suddenly, her stomach felt queasy. "Something light, maybe just a Caesar salad," she said as she closed the menu.

"Come on, you can eat more than that. I've seen you, remember?"

She laughed. "Okay, maybe a small pizza too. Can you help me with it?"

"No problem."

They ordered and the food came rather quickly. She chewed on the Romaine lettuce, enjoying the garlic flavour.

"I was thinking," said Sam.

"Umhum?"

"Well I don't really know your mother. We've never met and that's been no big deal to me. I've just been waiting for you to decide when to introduce me, and well, *now* with your mother's medical condition, it seems to be the right time."

Her stomach seemed to rise to her throat, and Emily stopped chewing and stared.

"I don't want to push you, but it would be nice if she knew who I was, don't you think?"

"Oh Sam, I don't know...I mean does it really matter?"

"Does it matter? Of course it does!" Sam looked incensed. "I'm a stranger to your mother. I just feel like such an outsider, you know?"

Why is he doing this now? She put her fork down. The last time a White guy came to her home was when she was 16. She had dated him a few times and he dropped by unexpectedly after his evening shift one school night. She tried to chat with him outside on the porch, but Dad came out with his hands on hips and glared at them the whole time. The boy left pretty quickly. After that, she made sure her boyfriends did not meet her parents. She looked at Sam. "Look, you don't get how my mom is about these things!"

"Get what? Like, I haven't figured out that I'm White and that isn't cool with your mom?" Sam said sarcastically.

She clenched her jaw and stared hard at the brown eyes looking at her. *How did he know?* "I am doing what is best for us because you don't know my mom!" her fist slammed down on the table.

Sam jerked back in surprise. "I'm sorry," he said raising his hands up. "It's just...well what if things turned for the worse and she never knows who I am?"

She thought of how warm and accepting Sam's parents had been of her. They already considered her to be family and bought her gifts at Christmas last year. Her face was flushed with embarrassment. She felt really stupid about her situation, but didn't know what else to do.

"Your parents don't know about my mother, right?" she demanded.

"No, of course not. I wouldn't say anything to anybody unless you said it's okay." He looked hurt.

"Sam, look..." she stammered as she wiped at the wetness on her cheeks.

"I'm sorry," said Sam as he grabbed for her hand. "I just wish I could be there more."

Emily tried to smile. "I know. My mother, you know, she's got these old- fashioned ideas that's all."

Sam sighed. "Let's just forget about it for now, okay?" He turned his attention to his pasta and began to eat.

Emily tried to finish her dinner, but had difficulty swallowing. She made an effort to eat half her food before they paid their bill and left. Sam put his arm around her as they walked back to her building. He pulled her close against him. Outside her apartment, Sam faced her to say goodnight.

"I'll call you tomorrow," he said and kissed her. "Everything okay?"

"I'm fine," she said as she tried to smile to hide her uneasiness.

That night, she tossed and turned as she dreamed of Sam meeting Ma. That incident on the porch when she was 16 didn't stop Emily. Now she knew she had to sneak around! Sometimes her dates dropped her off a block from home. Other times she let them park in the driveway for a quick goodnight kiss. Ma was always waiting up for her with that pout. She could see that exaggerated lower lip sticking out, arms folded across her chest, eyes glaring. Angry. Angry at what? What was she doing wrong? Weren't all the other girls going out on dates with boys? Good girls don't stay out late! White boys are bad! We kick you out! Ma would threaten. *Seriously?* She'd be thrown out and disowned? She heard that warning again and again. Nothing ever happened and she didn't really believe her parents would do that to her. *Or would they?*

Emily didn't start dating until she was 16. She had her share of crushes at school, but nothing seemed to develop. Some of her friends had boyfriends, but most of them were like her – chatting about boys, flirting but nothing serious. Things seemed to change in Grade 10.

Suddenly, everyone had a date for a high school dance or event. She reacted to the pressure by being the aggressor. *Why wait?* She found it much easier to ask a guy out then wait around to be picked up like some wallflower. During rebellious times, when she'd had an argument with her mother before going out, she'd make out parked on the street in front of the house. She never imagined her parents would knock on the car door when the windows were fogging up. *They never did.* In reality, she probably only kissed for a few minutes before her paranoia would set in and she'd cut it off. Strangely after these dates, her mother never said anything to her. To this day, she still didn't know if her mother's threat were real or not.

She woke up covered in sweat. It was 6:00 am. She went to the washroom to shower.

Somehow, Emily managed to get through the rest of the week without missing appointments or falling too far behind on reports. Ma had called on Friday to let her know that she had had the blood work done. She didn't know when her biopsy would be, but was told that Dr. Fung's office would call her on Monday about it. Emily rushed around her apartment to tidy up before Ma and Auntie Sue arrived. She'd already sent Sam home and wanted to make sure nothing suspicious was lying around. It was Saturday nine o'clock and their appointment with Dr. Lee was at 10:00. Just then the buzzer rang.

"Yes?" She answered the intercom.

"Emily it's us."

She pressed the buzzer to let them in, and opened the front door as she could hear their voices down the hall.

"Good morning," Auntie Sue and Ma said they came in the door.

"Good morning," she responded back with a smile. "Do you want some coffee before we go?"

Both women shook their heads. They had not moved from the doorway.

"Okay, we can go early." Emily grabbed her purse and locked up. She led the way to her car. "How are you feeling today, Ma?"

Ma shrugged her shoulders. "Same, but eating more. Getting fat with Auntie Sue's cooking."

Auntie Sue giggled. "I think your Ma is doing better. Yesterday she walked longer in the mall."

"Really?"

"Yes. We walked for almost half an hour before taking a break."

Emily looked over at Ma. She nodded her head and grinned. Her face seemed brighter.

In the car, it didn't take long before she was parking in Dr. Lee's neighbourhood. "Is it okay if we walk to the office? It's not too far."

Ma nodded. "Good exercise."

Ten minutes later, she opened the door to Dr. Lee's office. Inside, the same woman who had been in the office for treatment the day she consulted Dr. Lee was waiting. She looked at them and smiled.

"Have a seat," Emily said to her mom and aunt as she sat down.

Auntie Sue and Ma sat quietly as they looked around the office. They whispered to each other about the plants and paintings. A few minutes later the office door opened, and Dr. Lee came smiling into the waiting room. Ma and Auntie Sue leapt to their feet.

"Dr. Lee, this is my mother and my aunt," Emily said as she introduced them. They shook hands.

"Please have a seat. One minute, justa wait." He motioned to the other woman to come in.

They all sat down and watched as Dr. Lee led the other patient into his office and closed the door.

"We're next," Emily said reassuringly.

A short while later, Dr. Lee emerged and invited them into his office. Since there were only two chairs in his office, Emily opted to stand. Dr. Lee sat down, opened a blank file folder and wrote Ma's name across it. "Now what's the problem?"

"We discussed the problem the other day, remember?" she asked.

"Oh, yes," he said as he wrote. "Tell me how you are feeling?" he asked Ma.

Ma spoke to him in Chinese and told him about feeling tired and weak, coughing and not having much of an appetite to eat. He nodded and reached for her wrist to take her pulses.

"Liver, kidney, spleen, stomach, heart all very weak. Can do much to improve to make you stronger."

"What do you recommend?" asked Auntie Sue.

"Should do acupuncture, take herbs and take Chi Kung. Need all three to help, but expensive."

"How much?" Emily and her aunt asked.

"Chi Kung is $3000 for 12 sessions, acupuncture $35 each time and Chinese herbs have different costs."

She looked at her aunt. She had some money saved up, but wasn't sure if she had enough. "How many treatment do you recommend?"

"Two to three times each week for three months, at least."

"Expensive," Ma said and looked at Auntie Sue.

"Cost is okay," responded Auntie Sue without looking at Ma. "We have the money – what else are we going to do with it?" Ma protested in Chinese and they argued back and forth for a few minutes.

"I will pay," Ma insisted and looked at Dr. Lee. "My husband left me some money. I can help myself." Emily and Auntie Sue looked at each other.

Dr. Lee asked Ma to eat lots of fresh fish, then took out a box of vitamins. "I ordered these from California. Will also help you to get stronger to fight. Take one package each day."

"Are these good for Ma's condition?" Emily asked as she scrutinized the box.

"Yes. I consulted a doctor in San Francisco. Will help." He got up and went to the sink to wash his hands. "Emily, please take you mother to room number 2."

She led Ma and Auntie Sue down the hall to the treatment rooms. Each room had a narrow bed that resembled an examining table in a doctor's office, a chair and a small table. Auntie Sue took a seat and Ma lay back onto the bed. A knock was heard at the door and Dr. Lee came in with a handful of needles and a cotton ball. He asked Ma to open the lower part of her shirt and unzip her pants. Before he put each needle in, he swabbed the skin with an alcohol soaked cotton ball. He inserted needles in Ma's abdomen, legs, arms and neck. He then brought in a small machine to hook up to some of the needles for stimulation. Emily smiled as this used to be her job.

Once Dr. Lee left the room, she dimmed the overhead lights and motioned to her Auntie Sue. "Ma, you rest now. We will come back when your needles are ready to come out."

She closed the door and took Auntie Sue to a nearby coffee shop. They ordered two coffees and a muffin to share.

"How long for treatment?" Auntie Sue asked as she poured her third package of sugar into her cup.

"Usually 20 minutes. I don't know if she has to do Chi Kung today too."

"Oh. How long is that?"

"Another 40 minutes I think, I can't remember anymore." Emily broke a piece of muffin and placed it in her mouth. She pointed to the rest of it, and her aunt obliged by taking a piece.

"Good," her aunt said chewing in between sips.

"What do you think about Dr. Lee?"

"Seems okay."

"Have you heard about Chi Kung before?"

"Little bit. I read about it in the Chinese newspaper. Said it is good for all kinds of disease."

"Really?"

"You are doing a good job." Auntie Sue patted Emily's hand. "Don't worry."

After about 20 minutes, Emily returned to the clinic by herself to check on her mother. Auntie Sue remained in the coffee shop. Dr. Lee had just given her mother Chi Kung after taking out the needles.

"Come back in 40 minutes," he said as he closed the treatment room door.

She returned to the coffee shop. Auntie Sue was looking at the newspaper.

"You talk to Rachael?" she asked as she looked up.

"No. Not in a while." Emily tried to recall her last conversation with Rachael.

"Hmm. She has a new boyfriend, John. Nice guy. Has his own construction company."

"Oh." Emily avoided her aunt's stare and flipped through a section of the paper.

"He is Canadian." Auntie Sue continued, "but your uncle and I think that is okay."

Emily looked up surprised. "What do you mean Canadian?"

"Oh, I mean he is not Chinese but an Italian guy. His hair is a little long and he has lots of face hair!" Auntie Sue grimaced as she rubbed her chin.

She knows about this? Rachael never told her parents about dates. In fact, she used to give Emily ideas about how to sneak around. "So," she tested, "what do you think?"

Auntie Sue looked away. "Ai-ya, what can you do? You kids are all the same. You don't like Chinese boys, right?" she said in a sharp voice.

Emily sighed. "No, Auntie Sue, it's not that we don't like Chinese men, it's that we don't go out of our way to meet them."

"Same thing." Auntie Sue mumbled in Chinese.

"But would you accept this White guy?" She persisted.

"Of course! Have no choice." She shook her head, then added in a more hopeful voice, "Well, at least he has a good job."

Auntie Sue always seemed less old-fashioned compared to her mother. She bought her clothes instead of sewing them. She watched soap operas on television. She spoke to Rachael's friends rather than ignore them. Her English was better since she worked in the hospital cafeteria for 20 years. Still, Rachael stated that she would be "thrown out" if she dated any of the White boys at school. *Is she really okay with this construction guy?* Emily felt confused.

"Is it time?" Auntie Sue asked.

She nodded and they returned to the clinic. After Ma's treatment was done, Dr. Lee recommended that Ma go home to rest, and he showed her a Chi Kung walking exercise to do. Ma laughed as she tried to imitate him.

"Good, good," Dr. Lee said. "See treatment is helping already." They made their appointments for the following week and Emily drove them back to Auntie Sue's car.

When they arrived, Auntie Sue and Ma climbed into their automobile. "I have to go home and make these herbs for your Ma," Auntie Sue said motioning to the large bags of herbs Dr. Lee had given them. She urged Ma to fasten her seat belt and handed her a muffin to eat. They waved to Emily as they drove off.

Chapter Seven

On Sunday morning Emily woke with a start, as she jumped up and stared closely at the digital numbers on the clock radio. Without her contacts on, she had to move within a few inches of it and focus on one number at a time to read it. 9:15 am, oh my God! she thought as she dashed out of bed and into the bathroom. Yoga class was at ten o'clock. She had to hurry!

She had a quick pee, washed up, put her contact lenses in and clipped her hair back before marching back into her room to change into her workout clothes. She placed a clean top, jeans and makeup bag into her gym bag and ran out the door with an apple to eat. It was a cool, but bright April morning, and she walked briskly towards the subway station clutching at her lavender scarf and crunching on her Golden Delicious apple.

The warm air inside the subway helped her to shake off the cool spring air and she ran down the stairs to the subway platform. *What luck!* The white light of a southbound subway drew up. Empty pairs of beige and brown plastic seats with their backs together formed forward and backwards facing chairs. Between these groupings were more beige and brown chairs aligned in rows of three that lined the sides of the subway car. Emily preferred to face forward as it jostled her stomach less and took a seat by the window.

Once she arrived at her subway stop, she rushed out, leapt up the stairs by two and onto the street. *9:55, okay, I'm okay.* She walked into the gray stone building that hosted her yoga class. She took her shoes off in the hallway and put them beside a pair of brown loafers that looked like Jane's shoes. She walked straight into the classroom and towards Jane, who was seated on a blue yoga mat. The room was large, airy with 12-foot ceilings and multiple windows that let in the glory of the morning sun. She breathed in the ambient serenity and felt the muscles in her body muscles relax in reflex, yet taunt with expectation to fulfill. Emily grabbed a sticky purple mat, unrolled it beside Jane's and left her things at the back walls to ensure she had enough room to do all of her yoga postures.

"Hi," Jane with a smile.

"Hi," she replied.

"How's it going?" Jane asked.

Before Emily could reply, their yoga instructor walked in. "Good morning. Let's prepare for Sun Salutations."

They grinned at each other, got up and stood at the front of their yoga mats to begin.

After a challenging hour and a half workout, Emily and Jane gathered their things and went to the washroom to change. Emily looked at her face in the mirror, shiny with sweat and turned the faucet on. She splashed water on her face after Jane was done. The cool water felt like a slap against her hot skin, and she let it slide down her neck, before moping it up with a paper towel. Her dark eyes and round face contrasted against her friend's blue eyes and angular features in the mirror. She was so accustomed to seeing Jane's pretty face, not that Emily thought she wasn't attractive. *Just not in the typical way.* Refreshed and made up, she changed out of her clothes and into her jeans and t-shirt.

"Ready to eat?" Jane asked as she zipped up her black gym bag.

Emily nodded and they walked down the narrow flight of stairs to the main street. Outside they crossed the street to The Grill, the regular restaurant they went to after class for brunch. The place was busy. They took a seat at a small table at the front by the window, and Emily handed Jane a menu.

"Thank you," said Jane as she removed her light blue spring jacket. She had pulled her blonde hair back into a ponytail and patted the clips that held it in place.

"The usual?" Emily asked.

"Hmm...," said Jane. "I think so," as she looked at the menu.

They chuckled. Each week for the past year since they started their Ashtanga yoga classes, Jane and Emily had each ordered the same combination of poached eggs, pancakes, bacon and sausages. Emily preferred sausages with her egg and pancake combination, and Jane always ordered bacon with hers. It had become a joke between them.

Jane looked at her closely. "You okay?"

Emily nodded. "Let's order before we get into it, okay?" She had spoken to Jane a few times since she got the bad news about her mother, but she knew she'd have to explain the whole story to her. She wanted to avoid it.

Jane agreed. "I'm starved! How about you?"

She nodded as she looked at the food choices. She felt hungry and ordered the usual meal.

After they had placed their orders, Emily asked, "How is school?"

"Busy. I'm behind as usual." Jane relayed what she had to finish up even though school was technically over for the year. She had just completed the first year in her Master's of Social Work program and was working on her research proposal.

"Hold on. You're making my head hurt," Emily said grabbing her head.

"What about me? My head hurts all the time with the information I have to synthesize."

Emily smiled. She was always amazed at the way Jane could retain large pieces of information and somehow integrate it all for essays or research proposals.

"Problem is, I still need more information," Jane said as the food arrived. She cut into her eggs. "I just want a few more articles to support my position."

"You sure?" Emily asked as she laughed. "Maybe you have enough now."

Jane looked up skeptical. "Okay, maybe, but you know me."

They laughed. Emily and Jane had been roommates in their first year of university. Not only was Jane a brilliant academic, Emily discovered she was very skilled at flirting with men. Regularly on pub nights, men would try to join their table for drinks. Jane attracted a lot of attention with her blonde hair and full smile. She admired how easily Jane could flirt, yet somehow still sound smart. Emily found herself trying to emulate Jane in little ways. She'd try a few lines, laugh a little harder, even bought a top in a "Jane" colour. She was surprised by how easily men were lured by batting eyes. Some nights, she could carry on similarly to Jane; other nights, she got bored and reverted back to her former, more serious self, asking probing personal questions. To her amazement, Jane copied her behaviour some nights! They shared a lot of good times and bad times. She counted on her friend for support and she gave just as much back.

"I almost bought a bag of Oreo cookies, but I stopped myself!" laughed Jane.

"Oh, that neurotic eating!" Emily chortled, recalling their former late night studying habits.

"Okay, okay enough about school. Tell me about your mother. What's going on?"

Emily took a breath and then told Jane the story from the beginning to the treatment with Dr. Lee yesterday. She hoped Jane wouldn't be too analytical, as she had no more information to offer her than anyone else. As she spoke, she stared out the window and watched a young Asian woman about her age, helping an older woman to cross the street; likely it was her mother. The young woman smiled as she walked slowly across, letting her mother lean on her for support. It could have been her and Ma, but a different version of them. A happier version. She felt depressed and pissed off at the same time. *Wasn't that the image she'd always imagined of them?*

"Emily, are you okay?" Jane asked.

"What?" Emily turned her attention back to Jane, blinking to relax the tension around her eyes.

"You worked for this doctor after you graduated right?" Jane tried.

"Yeah, I did. So...what do you think?"

"I don't know that much about Chinese medicine, Em." Jane resumed eating, talking through her food. "But it doesn't sound like the family doctor is going to help you out much."

"Yeah, he's a real jerk," she agreed with a sigh.

"Can you see someone else without a referral note?"

"I'm not sure. Guess I could call and find out, eh?"

"I think I would call," replied Jane.

Emily agreed, losing her appetite as Jane shot out more and more questions. She didn't want to get upset. This was Jane. She was always helpful, but still Emily felt defensive.

At the end of the inquiry, Jane declared, "I'm sure this treatment with Dr. Lee will help in some way."

"You think so too? I hope so." Emily said reassured.

"I know so. And how is Sam with all this?" Jane probed.

"Good. He's been really helpful, but funny thing is, now with Ma being sick, he suggested I introduce him to her."

"Really? And...what do you think?"

"I don't know. I mean, I don't need Ma freaking out on me, you know?" Emily had shared her experiences with Jane about growing up and dating. Jane found her mother's behaviour "weird" and sometimes

89

reacted like Ma was almost too crazy to be true. *She never said this.* Emily could just tell by her facial expressions and body language. Jane always listened, but she knew Jane thought her mother would *never* disown her or throw her out. *What kind of mother threatens her child like that?* Maybe she was right, and Emily found herself sometimes daydreaming about a new kind of mother, although the fantasies didn't last. Ma usually found a way to just be Ma.

Jane nodded. "What are you going to do?"

She shrugged her shoulders. "Think my aunt was hinting that they know I am dating and maybe Ma would be okay with it."

"Oh?"

She told Jane what Auntie Sue had said to her at the coffee shop.

"That sounds encouraging, doesn't it?"

"Guess so."

"Why don't you bring Sam with you when you visit your mother next?"

"You think so?"

"You could say he's your friend. Give her something else to think about?" Jane's blue eyes danced happily, and her wiry grin looked suspiciously cat-like to Emily.

"Oh, I don't know," Emily moaned as she threw her head back. She was in no mood to deal with her mother's crazy antics. For all she knew, this could make matters worse.

"It's up to you, of course," replied Jane as she smiled into her coffee.

Chapter Eight

On Monday, Emily stopped for coffee before her assessment at 10:30. She pulled into the parking lot of the strip mall that had a Tim Hortons, got out and ordered a regular coffee and donut at the counter. She took a seat to eat her donut and pulled out her file to do a quick review of her next client's record. A few booths over were some young kids with their nannies eating donuts.

"Easy, easy," the Filipino woman said to the three kids, as they all grabbed for the yellow box of donuts.

"Okay, one at a time," the other nanny said as she helped to pass the box around.

Emily looked at the three kids. Guess there was no school today.

"Let's play war!" said the curly haired boy to his friend. "Hai-ya, hai-ya!" He yelled and waved a straw around.

The stocky boy laughed, got up, pulled a ruler out and started to whack at his friend's sister.

"Hey, stop that!" the girl yelled.

"Okay, you two sit down and finish your donuts first," instructed one of the caregivers who said something in Filipino to the other one.

"I *know* how to talk like Sharon," the blonde boy said staring at his nanny. "Duck a duck a ba ba beh." The other two kids giggled.

"Hey, that is rude," the two nannies retorted.

Emily felt flushed as she watched. She grabbed her donut and coffee and headed back to her car. From her car, she was unable to see the laughing kids, but heard an old childhood taunt, "Chinese, Japanese, dirty knees, look at these," in her head. So stupid, she thought to herself as she started the car and drove off to the assessment centre.

She rushed through the assessment, making very little small talk with her client. At the end of the appointment, she shook the client's hand, grabbed her belongings and hurried home. Outside her apartment door, her hand trembled as she tried to push the key into the lock. "Dammit!" she swore as the keys hit the floor. *Too much coffee.* She sighed as she picked up the keys and jerked the front door open. She walked straight into her home office and buried herself in work, typing up reports. She began feeling hungry as she neared the end of one of the last reports. It was 3:30. She had put the specialist, Dr. Smith's phone number on a neon-orange stick-it note and placed it on the bottom of her monitor. She pulled it off the bottom of her screen and picked up the cordless phone to call him. The line was busy again, like this morning. She pushed redial and waited.

"Doctor's office," a voice said.

"Yes," Emily said as she sat straight up. "Um, I was wondering how I could make an appointment for my mother to see Dr. Smith."

"Have we received a referral from your mother's doctor?"

"No."

"We need a referral from your mother's family physician, ma'am."

"Isn't there any other way to see him? Can't we pay him directly?"

"Dr. Smith doesn't work that way, ma'am."

"But my mother is dying of cancer, and her damned doctor won't send us for a second opinion!"

"I am sorry, ma'am, but the only way to get an appointment is through a physician's referral."

"Really?" Emily wiped a tear off her cheek.

"Yes.""

"Okay, thank you," she muttered as she hung up. She stared at the dead phone. *Now what?* She thought like the rehabilitation clinic she worked at, third party billing was possible for specialists. *Maybe Auntie Sue?* Perhaps her aunt could sweet talk Dr. Eng into making the referral? Her spirit lifted a bit, as she got up to find a snack.

The next day, Ma had another appointment with Dr. Lee. Emily arrived an hour after Ma's appointment time. Auntie Sue was reading a magazine in the waiting room and holding a white paper cup of coffee.

"Good morning, Emily," she said cheerfully. "Your Ma is inside." She pointed to the treatment rooms.

Emily let herself in through the door that separated the waiting room from treatment rooms and began walking down the hall. As she passed Dr. Lee's office, he looked up from his work and said: "Room 3. Acupuncture almost finished. Chi Kung next."

She nodded and stopped at the dark brown door with the number three on it. Dr. Lee had chosen black numbers with a gold background, which he stuck to the front of his six treatment rooms. She knocked softly and let herself in. The lights had been turned down to the lowest setting, but it was enough for her to see her mother's face. Ma's eyes were closed. She studied the wrinkles by her mouth. *Probably from pouting.* Ma's eyes flickered opened for a moment as she acknowledged Emily, then they closed again.

"Emily," she said softly.

"You okay, Ma?"

"Yes," she said.

Emily watched in silence as the acupuncture needles twitched along Ma's thin body. She turned when she heard a knock on the door and Dr.

96

Lee came in. He switched off the electrical machine, unhooked the wires attached to the needles and pulled out the needles from Ma's body. Next he took the long cigar-shaped herb and gave Ma moxibustion. Emily was never sure what moxibustion did, and she never dared apply it as close to the skin as Dr. Lee did.

"I come back to give Chi Kung," he said as he let himself out. Ma looked flushed from the treatment and began complaining about the bitter herbs she had to drink.

"Hey. Ma," Emily began. "What do you think of seeing a specialist in Toronto?"

"Another doctor? Ai-ya." Ma shook her head. "Too much trouble for your auntie!"

"But Ma, this might help you too."

Ma shook her head.

"But..." Emily started, but stopped as Dr. Lee stepped back into the room. "Forget about it, Ma," she said quickly. "Just close your eyes and forget about it." She watched Ma's forehead become smooth as her eyes closed again. Dr. Lee moved to the front of the bed to give her Chi. Emily walked out and passed her aunt in the waiting room. "I have to go to work, talk later?" Auntie Sue nodded.

Later that evening, Sam put the Styrofoam take-out containers away and led Emily to the couch after supper.

"So," he began. "What's been going on? You hardly said two words during dinner. Oh, and I wanted to ask you something as well."

Emily scratched her head and tugged at the shirt collar itching her neck. "Well, I didn't tell you but I spoke to Dr. Smith's office yesterday," she said. "But what is it that you wanted to ask me?"

"Oh, well I have this Chinese client and I wanted to ask you how to address him," Sam said. "But first tell me about what happened with Dr. Smith's office."

"What do you mean?" she asked coldly. "How to address him?"

"Yeah, you know, his last name is Wong, so how would you say Mr. Wong in Chinese?"

"Sam..." she began, "How would I know?"

"Oh," said Sam looking bewildered. "I just assumed that you knew how to speak Chinese because you told me your mom speaks to you in Chinese."

"I told you that I can understand Chinese, but it's a village dialect that no one speaks! I never said I could SPEAK Chinese!" she shouted.

"Okay, Emily," Sam said with his hands up. "It's no big deal! Let's get back to Dr. Smith, eh?"

"Chinese, Japanese, dirty knees, look at these," with vicious laughter rang through her head. She glared at Sam's brown eyes. *He's just like them.* Was Sam acting like those kids she saw earlier who made fun of their nannies? "Say something!" the neighbourhood kids use to taunt, mimicking Chinese words. She never gave in. She always ignored them and pretended it didn't bother her. Of course it really did, and it made her feel like an outsider.

Sam touched her arm. His face looked hurt. *Why am I being so stupid?* She regretted what she had thought earlier. Sam wasn't like those other kids! Yet, she felt guarded like she was in danger of being ridiculed. She focused herself to relay her conversation with Dr. Smith's office. "Okay," she said slowly. "We need a referral from the family physician, so I might as well give up."

"Why?"

"I told you about Dr. Eng!" she said exasperated. "He's all-knowing and he won't do it!"

"How can you be sure without asking him first?" Sam inquired.

"I already asked him and he said no!" she said as she stood up and paced around. "I mentioned the idea to Ma today too at the clinic, but she doesn't want to bother Auntie Sue anymore!"

"Why would it be a bother?" Sam asked confused.

"No, it's not a bother, it's just that Ma doesn't want to keep inconveniencing her," she said sternly. "I was going to ask my aunt to help me speak with the doctor, but not anymore."

"So, you won't ask your aunt about it?" Sam said slowly.

"I don't want to bother her like my mother said!"

Sam shook his head. "Look. Maybe if you go in with your aunt and talk with your mother's family doctor, he'll understand? What do you think? Don't worry about that other stuff – you're not bothering her."

How do I forget about the other stuff? She wondered. *Is this goi-law for real?* He didn't get it. She knew Sam didn't understand these silly cultural formalities, but she didn't want to have to explain it to him either. Besides what would she say? She didn't really get it either. She just knew she couldn't put her aunt out.

"This is crazy!" she yelled to no one in particular.

"Emily, can you lower your voice?" Sam said. "Geez, I don't understand this stuff. So are you're saying you don't want to set up an appointment with Dr. Smith?"

"You're not listening to me, Sam." Emily's pace quickened along the floor. She had lowered her voice, but wanted to find a way out of this conversation.

"Well, I am trying to!" he said loudly.

She stopped, shocked by Sam's tone of voice. *Sam never raises his voice.* She stared at his face. His brown eyes looked dim and small. *What am I doing? Why am I acting this way?*

"I know this all sounds silly to you," she said slowly. "I wanted to ask my aunt today for help, but then didn't feel I could." She stopped and turned away as she felt her body convulse.

""Okay...," he tried. "So maybe you can leave it for now?"

She folded her arms across her chest and nodded.

Sam stood up and wrapped his arms around her. She tried to pull away but he held on. Warmed, her body trembled as she felt her strength begin to melt away. *You're still here?* She grabbed onto Sam, buoyed by his strength.

"I'm stuck, Sam," she finally said. "I can't get any help from Dr. Eng, and I can't bother my aunt. Besides, Ma doesn't want to go."

"Okay, let's just leave it for now."

"You think that will be all right?" she asked hopefully as she turned to face him. "I can't force Ma to go, right?"

Sam looked down and nodded his head.

Chapter Nine

It was Mother's Day on Sunday and Auntie Sue's kids were planning on taking their mother out a day earlier to avoid the crowds.

"Why don't you join us?" Auntie Sue offered.

"I've got something special planned for Ma," Emily said secretly.

"Oh! She will be pleased." They decided that Emily would come over to Oakville Saturday afternoon and spend the night. While she was packing her burgundy Adidas bag, she wondered why she said what she said to her aunt and what special thing she was going to do. Taking her mother out to eat was the only thing she really did for fun with her. Then she noticed the unopened video of the *Joy Luck Club* on her bookshelf. She had picked it up on Boxing Day at one of the record stores for half price and toyed with the idea of watching it with her mother. As she stroked the plastic wrapping, she remembered sitting in the theatre, thankful for the dark. She hadn't brought enough tissue and struggled to unravel her last scrunched up piece. Jane had been sitting to the right of her crying off and on during the movie as well. She was touched by Jane's reaction to the movie and felt an even deeper bond with her, but was embarrassed by her own tears. She held the video and paused. She thought about how the main character in the movie became closer to her mother before she died. *Could we too?* Ma won't like this, she muttered as she studied the smiling actors' faces on the video. *Maybe?* She tucked it under her packed clothes impulsively, zipped up her bag and rushed out the door to pick her mother up.

In the car on the way back to Toronto, Ma repeated her concern about eating out.

"Don't worry, Ma! You know this restaurant has very fresh seafood. You told me this yourself."

"But Emily-a, Dr. Lee said don't eat out! Just buy fresh fish and eat every day."

Emily stared at her mother's unhappy face. When does this woman ever smile? she wondered.

Exasperated, she said, "Ma, what do you want me to do? Do you want me to call him?"

"No, no, don't disturb Dr. Lee, he is busy man," Ma said in protest.

"Look if you really don't want to go, I'll turn around now," she threatened and positioned the car to get off the highway.

"Okay, okay, almost there, right?" Ma said in a panic.

Emily nodded triumphant and accelerated. Fifteen minutes later, she exited the highway and drove through Markham's city streets towards her mother's favourite restaurant, the Best Wokk. It was 5:30, early enough to avoid the usual line up.

"See Ma," she said, "we don't have to wait; it's not busy." Emily was relieved.

Once inside, Ma studied the fish swimming in the tanks before taking her seat.

"The fish are fresh and the restaurant is clean," Ma announced out loud to no one in particular before she sat down.

"Ma," Emily said as she yanked at her mother's arm so she would sit. She felt hot and avoided the glances of the few patrons.

When the waitress came to their table, Ma ordered for them and asked repeatedly about the quality of the fish. Emily rolled her eyes. It's Mother's Day dinner, she said to herself over and over again to keep from reacting. Finally her mother seemed satisfied, she turned to Emily and asked, "Emily, you want some sweet and sour pork or something?"

"Okay, just sweet and sour pork," she agreed, salivating at the thought of her favourite dish. She took a sip of the hot tea. Ma preferred Chrysanthemum and always asked for it, even though she knew Emily didn't like it. She grimaced at the taste and reached down to make sure the gift was there. She had hidden the present in a plastic grocery bag, passing it off as fruit for Ma when asked about it. She stole a glance at her mother. *Now?*

"What is it?" Ma asked.

"Nothing, really," she murmured. Ma held her teacup to her lips and drank. Emily fidgeted in her seat. She felt anxious about her gift and she didn't know why. *Guess this is as good of a time as any.* She yanked the present out from the plastic bag.

"Well, actually I have this for you. Happy Mother's Day," she said as she placed the package on the table.

Ma put down her tea. "Pretty," she said as she touched the pink tissue paper and pink gift bag. "Very pretty."

Emily smiled and waited. She watched Ma toy with the tissue paper and squeeze at the bag, as if she was testing for fresh bread. Emily let out a sigh. "Go on, open it," she urged.

Ma pushed the layers of tissue paper aside, reached in and pulled out a black leather purse.

"Wow, leather?" she asked wide-eyed.

Emily nodded. This morning while she was still in Toronto, she had dutifully walked along Bloor Street, searching for her mother's present. She loved the black designer bag she saw at Holt Renfrew, but knew Ma could never appreciate it or its cost. Instead, she settled for a much cheaper, but still stylish mid-sized bag at The Bay. It looked nice and was on sale, something her mother would appreciate.

Ma pursed her lips, unzipped the bag and looked inside.

"It's big enough, right?" Emily checked.

"Expensive?" Ma asked as she closed it up. "Wow, Emily, you spend so much money?"

"No, Ma, not bad. Um...do you like it?" she asked hopefully.

"You spend *so* much money on me!" Ma said excitedly.

"Ma, really it wasn't that much money!" Emily lowered her voice and whispered, "Was expensive, but good price on sale."

Her mother beamed with approval. She was pleased with her success, but her smile quickly faded as she her mother emptied the contents of her old vinyl purse on the table. Some customers stared curiously at the assortment. Ma calmly put her lipstick, old compact, various gums and candies, nail clip, worn tissue package, wallet and an old indexed telephone book held together by a red elastic band into the new bag. "Everything fits," she said satisfied.

Emily blinked. *What did she say?* Her mother's lack of discretion was nothing new, conjuring up the familiar desire to disappear.

Ma continued to smile.

She paused for another second as she studied Ma's face. *She likes it?* She almost couldn't believe it since she felt so miserable.

Just then the waitress arrived with their fish and Emily quickly turned her attention to it.

"Look!" Ma said to the waitress. "My daughter bought this expensive purse for me!"

"Ma!" Emily cried. *It wasn't that expensive!* She looked at her mother who sat erect as a peacock, flaunting its fanned out colours. She felt her ears burn and she stared down at dinner. She recalled how Ma once arrived at her Grade 1 class during Show and Tell. Ma had suggested to her that she bring a pair chopsticks to class and demonstrate how to use them.

"But everyone else has brought in a book or toy to school," Emily whined, as she thought about the neat things the other kids brought in.

"Ai-ya!" said Ma. "There are no other Chinese kids in your class right?"

"Yes..."

"So, this is a good chance to show them goi-laws about Chinese people!" Ma said proudly, handing her a pair of plastic chopsticks.

"O...kay," Emily agreed slowly taking the sticks from her mother's hand.

Ma smiled and went back into the kitchen to clean up the breakfast dishes.

"Hey, Emily," a voice called from the front door.

"I'm coming," she answered, quickly dropping the chopsticks behind a pillow on the couch.

"I'm going Ma," Emily called out with a stuffed elephant tucked under her arm. She raced out the door and hopped and skipped along to school with her friends. Right after singing O Canada, it was Show and Tell. Emily squeezed at the fuzzy animal on her lap, anticipating her name to be called. Instead, there was a knock on the door. Mrs. Johnson, the teacher, opened it. Ma was standing at the doorway with the white plastic chopsticks in her hand. Emily dropped her elephant to the ground and sank down into her desk, trying to hide from her mother.

"Isn't that your mother?" Bobby sneered in her ear from behind.

"Emily-a," Ma said as she walked right up to her desk and put the chopsticks in front of her.

"Mrs. Chow has brought Emily's Show and Tell item," said Mrs. Johnson to the class with a smile. "Emily why don't you come to the front and demonstrate for us?"

Her legs felt heavy, like she had just run around the gym ten times. She was sure she was flushed and as red as the apple she just walked past on Mrs. Johnson's desk. She clutched at the smooth sticks. Ma had moved to the right side of the classroom by the door and was grinning from ear to ear. Emily turned around to face the class and shot a glance at her mother. *Leave.* Ma just stood still and waited.

She let out a sigh and looked down to position the sticks in her right hand. She held the top stick between the middle finger and forefinger, keeping the thumb up to hold it in place. The bottom chopstick was the base and she tried to lay it straight across her ring finger and the gap between her thumb and forefinger. Gingerly, she moved the top stick down to hit the front of the base stick.

"Pick up something," Ma called with a smile.

A pink eraser was on Mrs. Smith's desk, so she raised the top chopstick again and tried to grip the eraser between the sticks. She felt her hand cramp as she held on tightly and lifted the eraser into the air.

Mrs. Johnson began to clap and the class clapped along.

Despite herself, she grinned at the class and took her eyes away from the chopsticks.

"Plunk" the eraser fell to the ground. A couple of boys started to laugh. In horror, she quickly knelt down to pick it up. When she straightened up, Ma was standing beside her. She took the chopsticks from Emily's hands and began to walk around, lifting objects off of everyone's desks with them. Emily stared at her mother who was proudly walking from desk to desk. Most of the kids were laughing, but

Ma didn't seem to notice. She just continued up and down the rows, until she was finished.

"Nice purse," the waitress said as she smiled at her mother. Other patrons turned to look, and Ma held it up like a trophy.

"Stop it, Ma!" Emily whispered, as she firmly pushed her mother's arm down and put the purse away. *Why does she have to act this way?* She was conflicted. Pleased her mom liked the present, but embarrassed by her childish behaviour.

"Let's eat!" she commanded and hung the new purse up. She served her mother some fish before putting some on her plate.

Ma stared at her food with a jutted lower lip.

I know what that means. Emily ignored the message that Ma was upset and picked up a small piece of steamed pickerel, dipped it back into the soy sauce and oil surrounding the main fish and placed it in her mouth. She chewed slowly, deliberately to ensure there were no bones before adding more rice to her mouth when the fish was sufficiently melted.

"It's fresh, eat more!" Ma encouraged as she ate.

She picked up another small piece.

"Ai," said Ma shaking her head. "Ever since you small girl and you choke on that fish bone, you haven't eaten fish!"

"I eat a little!"

"Fish is good for you. Even Dr. Lee said so!"

She opened her mouth to respond, but paused as the waitress placed a plate of hot sweet and sour pork and snow pea leaves in front of her. Seduced by the steamy garlic and tangy smells, she served her mother first, before she put a large serving of food onto her own plate. Ma also concentrated on her food. It didn't take long for Emily to feel content by the fullness in her belly.

"Have some of my rice," Ma offered from her half-eaten bowl.

"Okay," she said as she filled her empty one. "But you finish the rest," she said as she handed her back a small amount of rice.

Ma nodded and continued to eat.

They continued in silence soothed by the wonderful food. After Emily finished all of her rice, she put her chopsticks down and looked over at her mother, who had also stopped eating and was asking the waitress for take-out containers.

"You ate better, Ma," she commented.

""Yes, I seem to be getting my appetite back," Ma said pleased.

"That's good," Emily said looking at Ma's pink cheeks. "You've been enjoying yourself with Auntie Sue?" she inquired.

"Yes, good," Ma said brightly.

"Lots to talk about, gossip?"

Ma covered her mouth and giggled like a schoolgirl.

What do they talk about? She wondered, recalling how her mother and aunt could get lost in conversation and ignore everyone around them. She looked around at the other tables. Happy families sitting together smiling. She looked at Ma. She was also smiling but seemed far away. *I'm not smiling.* She picked up the plastic spoon that came with the red bean dessert soup and continued sadly. "You and Auntie Sue?" Ma just nodded. She guessed there wasn't much else to say about it. Auntie Sue and Ma were close; she and her mother weren't.

The restaurant was getting busier and noisier. She looked up from her food and noticed a mixed couple had been seated across from them. Ma was staring. From her line of vision, she could see her mother's pout. *Good God. Auntie Sue is so wrong about Ma!* She quickly finished up her soup and took some cash out to pay the bill. "Ready?" she asked.

Ma nodded and got up. She followed behind to avoid conversation, carrying the leftover food and Ma's old vinyl purse now hidden in the pink gift bag. Ma stopped suddenly and she stepped up to see what was wrong. Just as she was going to ask, she felt her mother take hold of her arm and moved forward. Bewildered, she walked arm and arm with Ma, past the crowd and out the door.

Chapter Ten

Sunday after lunch, Emily gathered her belongings up and placed them back in her bag, on top of the unmoved video. When they returned home after dinner last night, Ma wanted to watch some Chinese show, so Emily got her book out to read. She toyed with the idea of bringing the movie out, imagining the two of them crying and laughing together. An hour or so later, Ma was asleep on the couch. The opportunity was gone and she didn't feel like watching the flick alone after Ma had gone to bed. Besides, her mind was riddled with thoughts about that mixed couple. *Why was she pouting? What would she say to us?* She shook the thoughts away and tried to concentrate on the television show. Eventually she passed out on the couch and dragged herself up to bed sometime after midnight.

Emily checked her makeup one last time, before descending the stairs with her gym bag. Ma was in the kitchen preparing some more herbs.

"I've got a lot of work to do," she fibbed. She moved closer to her mother. *Should I?* She quickly pecked Ma's cheek and moved a safe distance away. She didn't know how her mother would react, but she felt flushed like she might be doing something wrong. Her mother just smiled. Emily turned away to hide her blush.

"Don't worry. Auntie Sue be back at dinner time, and I have soup to make," said Ma.

Emily smiled and waved as she walked out the door. She glanced at her watch as she pulled away from the house. Lying had become second nature for her. It was 2:00 and she was due at Sam's parent's house by 3:00. Traffic was heavy on the highway, with cars filled with people and families. Mother's Day brought everyone out to some destination it seemed. She drove bumper to bumper, until she finally saw the exit sign for Park Lawn Street. It was 2:45.

Exiting the highway, she drove north in a single lane as parked cars lined the street to tall multi-dwelling homes. Narrow steps, too many to count, led from the gray concrete sidewalk up to the homes. On the west side of her was High Park, with its large oak trees, maple trees, zoo and amphitheatre that she and Sam went to last summer. They had brought ham sandwiches and cold corn on the cob to eat, as their backs stiffened from sitting on the hard grassy hill, watching Twelfth Night. Emily drove past the park and Bloor Street, twisted and turned through residential neighbourhoods until she came up to a large two storey white house. White shutters framed the gleaming windows and golden brass numbers 222 were centred on the blue wooden door. She walked up the concrete slab stairs to the door, lifted the heavy brass doorknocker and let it slam down twice. It was 3:30. Her lips felt dry and she realized she had forgotten to reapply lipstick.

"Why hello, Emily!" Mr. Taylor said with a smile as the door opened. He offered her his right hand and gave it a stiff shake.

"Mister...a Bob," she said as she disengaged her hand. Mr. and Mrs. Taylor had asked her to call them by their first names. She found this easier with Sharon, Sam's mom.

"Sam, Sharon," he turned and called. "Emily's here!"

Sam came up from behind his dad's shiny head. He put his hands on his dad's shoulders and beamed. Then he bent towards her and gave her a quick kiss on the cheek. Emily flushed as his mother came from the living room, adjusting her gold-framed glasses on her slightly crocked nose and smiled. Her hair was styled similarly to her mother's and all women from that generation: short and curled from being set in rollers. Sam shared his mom's large nose and lanky limbs. He was sporting a spotty beard since he had not shaven. It had prickled against her skin from his peck and she rubbed at her irritated skin. She glanced at Sam, who had stopped smiling. *Damn he noticed.* Remembering the pot of flowers she brought, she scooped it up and offered it to Sharon.

"Happy Mother's Day," she said. Her voice reverberated down the hallway.

"How thoughtful! Thank you Emily," she said as she wrapped her tree-like limbs around her.

Emily put her arms around Sharon's back. She felt awkward, but patted her back a few times until Sharon set her free. Sharon and Bob reminded her of Jane's parents.

"Let me find a place for these," she said. Sharon and Bob turned and walked towards the kitchen, leaving Emily and Sam behind standing in the hallway. Sam grabbed Emily's hand and held it to his chest.

"I'll shave before dinner," he said.

"Okay, thanks," she said.

He bent down to kiss her, but she drew away and looked at the kitchen for signs of Bob and Sharon. She stared at Sam's wiry grin. *Why is he always so affectionate when he's here?*

"Stop worrying about my folks," he said with a chuckle. "I'm glad you're here," he added.

"Have you been having a good weekend?" she asked.

"Yeah. Dad and I worked on his garden yesterday, and mom and I went to a movie last night."

"That sounds nice. Where's your sister?"

"She's visiting a friend and should be here any minute to help with dinner."

"Is there anything I can do to help?"

"Nope, everything is under control. Dad's going to barbeque salmon tonight, and Chris and I have the salad planned out."

"Sounds great."

"And how was your time with your mom?"

"Oh, okay," Emily said. "Uh...maybe I should see if your mom needs any help?"

"Sounds good. I'll go up to do my business," he said rubbing at his face.

She smiled as she watched Sam bounce up the stairs like a deer. Her facial muscles ached and she let them relax, happy for the break. After Sam was out of sight, she strolled over to the kitchen and found Bob mixing drinks for himself and Sharon.

"Would you like something, Emily?" he asked.

"No thanks," she said.

"Are you sure?"

"Okay, just some juice, but I can help myself."

She poured herself some orange juice and followed behind Bob and Sharon as they moved into the family room. Sharon sat down on the couch; Bob kept walking, golden liquid in hand through the next doorway and into his den. Sam called this a leftover social ritual from the 50s: 4 pm cocktails before dinner. Just as she sat down opposite Sharon on the couch, Sam sprung into the family room, beer in hand and sat in the middle between the two women. The patchwork was gone from his face.

"Like a baby's bottom," he laughed touching his face.

She grinned and reached up to feel the softness, but withdrew her hand when she noticed Sharon watching. She turned her attention to the news on the television. Everyone stared straight ahead. Emily drank in the cold, tangy liquid, happy to let the noise box chatter. About ten minutes later, Christine burst into the room, wineglass in hand, shattering the calm.

"Hey, Emily!" Christine called. She stopped in front of her and hugged her with the one free hand. "Do you want some wine?"

Emily hugged her back, smiled and replied, "No, I think I'll wait till dinner."

"So how was dinner with your mother?" she asked.

"Fine. Yeah, we had a nice time."

"Where did you take her?"

"Oh to her favourite Chinese restaurant."

"Hmm... sounds good. We should try it sometime, eh mom?"

"Sure," Sharon replied, then whispering to Emily, "Bob doesn't like Chinese food, but I do! We'll go." She smiled and winked, motioning that the three of them go secretly.

Emily felt pleased and looked forward to planning their secret dinner.

"So, let's get to it," Christine said to Sam as he stood up.

"Okay,"" he said as he followed his sister into the kitchen

"Can I help?" Emily called after them.

"No, we have things under control. Just relax here with mom," Sam said as he poked his head back around to the living room to answer her. He smiled, before going back into the kitchen.

Emily smiled at Sharon who was sitting on the opposite end of the floral couch. She looked at the fireplace in front of her: cleanly sweep with no sign of dirt or ashes present. An upright piano stood against the wall to the right of her, and a large photo of Bob's father was mounted over it. Sharon had resumed her needlepoint and glanced at her with a smile as she watched.

"What are you making?" she asked.

"Oh this is for one of the living room pillows on the sofa," she replied.

"Hmm."

"I've completed one already. You can see it if you like. I put it back on the sofa already."

"Sure," she replied rising, eager to please. She marched straight past the staircase and over to the living room. A stiff looking blue couch and loveseat furnished the unused front of the room, while a large oak dining table and buffet stood at the opposite end of the room past the French doors. She picked up the beige pillow with the newly sewn cover and stroked the flowerpot design. It was perfectly sewn. Outside through the large bay window, she could see how bright the blue sky was.

"Hey watcha doing?" a voice called.

Emily started and turned to find Sam with dinner plates in his hand, standing at the entranceway of the kitchen and dining room.

"Just admiring your mom's handiwork," she said with a smile.

"Yeah, she's really into it. It's good for her, you know? Keeps her busy."

Emily nodded and added, "Do you need a hand?"

"Sure," he said and they set the table together.

Dinner was ready at five o'clock sharp, as Bob had announced earlier. She was seated beside Sam, who gave her hand a squeeze as the family gathered at the table.

"Dear, why don't you say Grace?" Bob asked.

"Thank you," Sharon replied and launched into a prayer.

Emily looked down at her hands to give the appearance of praying. She remembered standing beside her desk in public school as the principal's voice boomed through the PA system every morning. After *O Canada*, the Lord's Prayer was usually recited. Kids who talked or who didn't bow their head were given a stern look by the teacher and sometimes taken aside afterward for a little "chat." She had no idea what this praying stuff was about, but she was a fast learner. Most kids in class told the teacher they went to the United Church. Sounded good to her, so she learned to say the same thing. In fact, she taught herself so well that when Bob asked her what church she belonged to she said, "United" before she could stop herself. Bob responded with a satisfied smile, and she grinned back thankful her answer was enough for him.

"Amen," Sharon said with Bob, Sam and Christine chorusing after her. She looked up on cue and smiled.

Sam raised his wine glass, "Happy Mother's Day." Emily picked up her wine glass and joined in. Since that embarrassing first date, she tried to avoid drinking much alcohol. Sam knew this and had poured water in her glass. She clinked glasses with the others, happy that she was blending in.

After eating dinner, watching the news and cleaning up the kitchen with Sam's family, Emily helped Sam pack up his belongings in his old bedroom. A small wooden desk sat in front of the bedroom windows that faced the front of the house and his single bed was on the adjacent wall. Sam sat and jerked his body up and down on the bedsprings of his bed. He pulled her closer, motioning for her to give it a try. She sat down and they bounced alternatively on the old box spring and laughed.

"Sam," Sharon called from the stairwell.

"Yes, Mom?" Sam stopped and walked to the open doorway of the bedroom.

"Will you be leaving soon?"

"Yep. Emily is just helping me pack."

"Okay. Do you want me to pack you some leftovers?"

"Sure, Mom." Sam turned back and rolled his eyes at her. He whispered, "She's checking up on us."

Emily nodded and smiled. "You want me to go downstairs?"

"Nah, she has to learn to relax, you know?"

She smiled, but decided to sit on the blanket box at the opposite end of Sam's room.

"Where ya going?" Sam asked with a laugh.

"I can see you better from here," she said.

"Sure, okay Em," Sam said shaking his head.

She smiled, feeling quite safe on the firm wooden box. Below she could hear the echo of Sharon's footsteps as she moved from the kitchen to the family room. "Spying" Sam would say. She didn't get his parents. They seemed so open. Sam discussed topics she would never dream of mentioning to her mother! She even had a few "adult" conversations with Sharon, like what it's like to be an artist, how some kids become street kids and other topics from the newspaper that Sharon chose to discuss with her. It was so refreshing, unlike her lectures from her mother, and she felt grateful to be able to share her opinions without any screaming or obvious repercussions. Yet, they had their rules too, the most important one being "no sex in the house." Sam complained about this on their first visit to his parents's home.

She didn't get why he hated this rule. *Don't all parents have rules?* Emily had no intention of upsetting Sharon, so she tried to limit any open affection. Sam acted more endearing in front of his parents, causing her to feel very self-conscious. She wasn't aware of how hell bent he was to break this rule, until she stayed over last month for Easter weekend. Right after dinner, his parents left for a bridge game. Sam practically carried her up the stairs, after he watched their car drive away.

"Are you sure?" she cautioned, staring out his open bedroom door.

"Don't worry, they're gone," Sam said assuring her as he rapidly undressed her.

Emily couldn't stop staring out the open doorway. She felt frigid as Sam pushed her legs apart and started thrusting his tongue around.

"Sam, we shouldn't," she said, wanting to push him away, but instead found herself strangely excited. He moved in quickly, causing her to moan out with pleasure.

Suddenly, the front door opened and they both froze.

"Sam," Bob called out. "I just forgot to take this travel brochure with me."

"Okay, Dad," Sam yelled back casually, winking down at Emily's fearful face.

Bob paused in the hallway. "Is everything okay?" he asked.

What's he doing, what's he doing? Emily felt her heart pound into Sam's chest.

"Sure, Dad," Sam replied. "We're coming right down to watch a movie."

"Great! I'm off," Bob said.

Emily waited for the door to close before she thought she could breathe again.

"Now, where were we?" Sam asked playfully.

"Nowhere!" Emily retorted, pushing him off her.

"Oh come on, Em! He's gone! I think you're ready for round two..." he said as he tried to kiss her cheek and stroke her thigh.

"Enough, already!" she said putting on her clothes. "We could have been caught, don't you think?"

Sam laughed. "Yeah, I would have loved to see my dad's face!"

Seriously? She stared at his snickering face in disbelief. *Idiot.* She turned and walked down the stairs to go to the family room.

"Emily! Come back!" Sam called.

She turned on the television, madly searching for something to watch. Sam appeared in the doorway, fully dressed and moved slowly to the couch. She turned her back to him as he sat down. *Jerk.*

"Emily," he said as he touched her back.

She leapt to the opposite end of the couch.

"Look," Sam said with a sigh, "I'm sorry. It's just, well I guess it's always been my boyhood fantasy, you know? Have sex in my parents' house..."

"Don't you think your dad knows?" she demanded.

"Maybe..."

"He'll probably say something to your mother, you know," she cussed.

"Don't worry. They don't know!" he tried.

"Okay, so why did your dad ask 'if everything was okay?'"

Sam sighed. "Okay, maybe he was suspicious but I'll take care of it, don't worry!"

Emily crossed her arms and fixated on the television screen. Sam had ruined everything for her. *What would Sharon think of her now?* She ignored him for the rest of the night and went upstairs later without saying goodnight. The next morning, at breakfast, a perky Sharon chatted about her bridge game and didn't ask anything about their evening, except how the movie was. She was dumbfounded. *Maybe Sam was right and they didn't know?* She felt unsure and worked harder to please Sharon.

"Okay, I'm all done," Sam, announced, disturbing her thoughts. He had made his bed and had slug his duffel bag over his right shoulder.

Emily looked at his sailor-like stance and saluted. "Aye, aye. Let's go," and proceeded to march down the stairs. Sam laughed and chased her down, grabbing to tickle her at the waist. She raced ahead, stopping abruptly as Sharon and Bob rounded the corner to meet them at the bottom of the stairs.

"Hi, Sharon. Hi, Bob," she said a bit out of breathe.

Sam swooped down and grabbed her by the waist. "Hey, Mom and Dad!"

She felt flustered and tried to move away, but Sam he held on tight.

"Thanks for a great weekend," Sam said and he gave each parent a hug.

"Yes, thanks for dinner. It was great," she said breaking Sam's grip to give Sharon a light embrace. Bob gave her a firm handshake.

"Great to see you," Sharon said. "Come back anytime."

Emily beamed.

They walked out the door and towards her car. Outside, with the front door safely shut, Emily drank in his soft lips for a deep kiss.

"Gotta get going," she said as the bright moonlight awakened her eyes.

"Yeah, we'd better start driving," he replied. "Do you want me to come over?"

"Yes, but...I should do some work and get to bed early."

"Okay, Hon," he said giving her another small peck. "I'll come by after work," he said walking backwards towards his car. "Call me tonight when you get home, so I know you arrived safely, okay?" he said.

"Sure," she said as she got into her car, started it up and drove away. She turned on the radio and hummed to herself as she drove.

Chapter Eleven

On Monday the sun felt warm as she dropped by Dr. Lee's clinic to see how her mother was progressing. Mid-season tulips were now blooming and buds seemed to have burst on trees and bushes covering their once bare limbs with green modesty. She entered the clinic to find Ma walking and smiling and Dr. Lee clapping.

"Look Emily!" Dr. Lee said happily, "your Ma can do Chi Kung walking exercise very good now!"

She watched as Ma took wide exaggerated steps.

"Getting stronger!" Dr. Lee exclaimed.

"How do you feel Ma?" she queried.

"Better. More energy," Ma replied.

"Really? That's great!" she said, noting Ma's rosy looking cheeks.

"Your ma surprised me today," Auntie Sue added. "She got up before me, had breakfast and was doing this walking exercise when I came downstairs!"

Ma giggled and nodded as she looked at Dr. Lee who smiled back at her like a proud father.

"Okay, go home now, rest and take more medicine." Dr. Lee instructed as he handed Ma her herbs for brewing.

"Do you want to come over?" Emily asked as she helped Ma with her jacket. "I could pick up some lunch?"

Auntie Sue shook her head. "I've got some soup at home for your mother, and we'll heat up the leftover fish and vegetables from last night's dinner for lunch."

"Okay," she said softly, surprised by the disappointment in her voice.

"If you have time, come over for supper," Ma said outside the clinic.

She agreed and they parted to walk to their separate parked cars. On her way home, she pulled into a McDonald's drive-through for some lunch. She walked quickly from her car into the apartment building, munching on crispy hot French fries as she ascended the stairs to the first floor of her building. She pulled the heavy double glass doors to the entranceway open and used her key to open her mailbox. She flipped through the three pieces of junk mail as she walked back to her apartment.

Inside, Emily stepped out of her black loafers, noticed the grease dotting the brown and red McDonald's bag she had been holding and placed it along with the mail onto the kitchen counter. Opening the take-out bag, she munched on some French fries and took a plate out for her lunch. As she sat down, she thought again about Dr. Smith. She hadn't fully given up on the idea of her mother going to see him for a consultation. *It couldn't hurt, right?* Yet, she didn't know what to do about Dr. Eng. Maybe Auntie Sue wouldn't mind? She pondered. Private clinics existed in the United States, but what was she going to do? Drag her mother down there? She also didn't remember when Dr. Smith's office even had an opening for an appointment. She decided to call again.

"Doctor's office," responded the voice.

"Oh hello," she said recognizing the same person. "It's Emily Chow. I think I spoke to you the other day about getting a second specialist opinion for my mother?"

"Yes?" She sounded impatient.

"I forgot to ask you when the next opening is to see the doctor?"

"We need a medical referral, ma'am."

"Of course," she said playing along. "I think my mom's doctor plans on faxing the referral today, but I have to be present to interpret for my mother. It would be so helpful if I knew in advance when the next opening is."

"Is it urgent?" she asked.

"Yes, very urgent," she said with authority.

"Well, I have an opening this Friday due to a cancellation, but I would need that referral immediately."

"Can you hold it for us?" she asked anxiously. "I'll look into it right away. Please just give me a bit of time, like an hour or something."

"We don't normally hold appointments open, Ms. Chow."

"Please! I'll call the moment we hang up and get back to you!" She tried to keep her voice calm, but felt desperate.

There was silence on the other end of the phone. "I have some paperwork and calls to make for about an hour, but after that, I have to deal with this," she said.

"Thank you, thank you," Emily said as she hung up. She needed to get Auntie Sue on board, but she called Sam and explained that situation.

"I'm not sure what to do. My mother looked so happy today at Dr. Lee's clinic. She was walking and she told Auntie Sue that she was getting stronger. Even Auntie Sue looked pleased!"

"Really?"

"I mean, I don't want to upset her, you know? And what if Dr. Eng is right? I mean I can't stand that guy, but I know Ma would hate all the tests and stuff, you know?"

"I don't know what to tell you, Em," Sam said.

"Yeah, I...I'm not sure either." She moved the phone away from her ear to shift the pressure she felt and sighed out loud.

"I don't know, Em," Sam started. "Why don't you speak with your mother or your Auntie Sue about it?"

"Yeah, I guess I should speak with Auntie Sue. If she thinks it is a good idea, she has to get that referral and convince Ma to go."

"Sounds like the best route to try," said Sam.

"Okay. I'll call her and let you know what we decide. Does that sound okay?"

"Of course, Em. Don't worry; you are doing all that you can for your mother."

He's so sweet. She felt her shoulder tension ease for a second and found herself breathing a bit deeper. "Thank you Sam," she said and hung up. She dialed home immediately and Ma answered the phone.

"Hello?"

"Hi Ma, it's me. Have you eaten yet?"

"Yes, just finish lunch. How about you, you eat yet?"

"Yes, well sort of...it doesn't matter, I just wanted to check on you and make sure everything is fine."

"Yes, I feel good," Ma said in a surprised voice, then added, "don't worry so much! I *am* feeling stronger. I was talking to your aunt about a trip, a cruise or something."

"What? Really Ma?" she said. Ma always complained vacations were a waste of money!

Ma laughed. "Yes, I was reading about one for seniors in the Chinese newspaper. Did you want to speak with Auntie Sue?"

"A...sure," she said. She envisioned Ma and Auntie Sue on a cruise ship with Ma doing Chi Kung walking. *Is Ma really getting better?* .

"Hello Emily?"

"Oh...hi Auntie Sue." *Why did I call?* She paused. *Oh yeah that doctor.* "A...hey, can you move to a room where Ma can't hear you? I want to speak to you in private."

"Why, is everything okay?" her aunt whispered.

"Yes, yes, well I have to ask you something, that's all."

"Okay, wait while I make some excuse."

Emily listened as her aunt teased her mom about her appetite and then urged her to go take a nap to fatten up some more. After a few minutes, she heard her aunt's slippers clack back down the stairs.

"Okay, she has gone for a nap now. What is it? Is there something wrong?"

"No, I just want to make sure everything is okay, that's all."

"Oh," her aunt sounded relieved. "I think so. She is eating more and doing more. We went to the mall yesterday, and she didn't seem to get as tired as before. Then she brought up this idea of a cruise," she laughed.

"Yeah, she mentioned going on a vacation with you just now."

"That's great, huh?" Auntie Sue laughed. "So many times I asked her to go before. Always she said no. Now, she is Chi Kung walking and we are going to plan a trip!"

"I'm happy to hear that..." Emily said as the same cruise ship image appeared.

"I think Dr. Lee is really helping her, Emily!"

"Yeah...I think so too...but...um..." *What is Chi Kung walking anyways?* She wondered to herself.

"So what is it, Emily?"

"Oh, um...what do you think about seeing other doctors? You know the Western doctors?" Her heart pounded hard.

"What do you mean?" Auntie Sue sounded confused.

"Well, you remember that doctor that I took Ma to? Dr. Fung? He was a specialist, but he didn't want to treat Ma."

"You mean the doctor who asked us to take more of your mother's blood?"

"Yes, that one!"

"But I thought you didn't want to see that doctor?"

"Yes, you are right. That doctor said he cannot help Ma, but I found another one in Toronto who might be able to help Ma."

"Really? How? Did Dr. Fung help you?"

She paused for a second. Sam's face flashed through her mind. *Should I?* She closed her eyes and blurted, "My boyfriend's cousin is a doctor, and he said this doctor in Toronto is very good."

"You have a boyfriend?" Auntie Sue whispered delighted. "I knew it! Why don't you tell your ma? When can we meet him? You know she worries about you not having a boyfriend."

"Yes, yes, can we talk about that later?" Emily asked impatiently.

Auntie Sue acted like she did not hear her. Instead, she launched into a series of questions, that Emily knew she would have to answer.

"You are right, he is not Chinese," she said as she rolled her eyes. And, "yes, he has a good job, he is an accountant." Even though Auntie Sue sounded happy and excited, Emily was tense and leery of her questions. She was certain Ma's voice would boom through the speaker and accuse her of being a *naughty girl for not listening to her mother!* After some more probing questions, she cut her aunt off, saying, "Auntie Sue, quit bugging me! I didn't call you to be interrogated!"

Auntie Sue did not respond.

Why did I do that? "I'm sorry, Auntie Sue, I didn't mean to shout," she said ashamed of her childish reaction. "I just need to speak to you about this specialist, okay?"

"Okay, okay Emily." Her aunt did not seem hurt. "What do you think we should do?" she continued.

"I don't know," Emily said thankful for her aunt's response. "Do you think Ma would go see someone else?"

"Sure...well maybe. I guess it all depends – does she have to go to a hospital, because she really doesn't like hospitals."

"Yes, this doctor's office is in a hospital."

"Hmm." Auntie Sue sounded skeptical.

"She would probably have to do some more blood tests and things like that."

"Oh no! She won't like that at all! And will she have to do cancer treatment?"

"I guess so..."

"Oh Emily, your ma seems so much happier right now and she seems stronger."

"Yeah, she did seem better today," she said agreeing with Auntie Sue. She thought again of her mother's smiling face today. Suddenly she imagined Ma's pouty, sullen face during chemotherapy or radiation treatment. Could she handle seeing that face on Ma? Maybe Dr. Lee was really helping? Auntie Sue was silent. No one wanted to upset her mother. Resigned, she finally said, "Well, I guess we could wait on this a bit longer..."

"Yes! I think that is a good idea!" Auntie Sue seemed satisfied.

"Okay, Auntie Sue. Thanks for all your help again," she said as she hung up the phone. She considered again her mother's happy face and the surety in her voice that she was getting better. *Maybe she is?* She really didn't know, but she was certain she couldn't face that pout on her mother's face from chemotherapy or radiation treatment. Left with no other option, she called Dr. Smith's office to let them know she wouldn't need the appointment. After she hung up, she stared at the phone blankly. She had closed the door now on Western medicine. She was surprised to feel almost like a relief in this decision. *Was Dr. Lee really a healer?* She didn't know, but knew they were committed to this

Chinese medicine path. To quiet her misgivings, she channeled her energy into work.

That evening, Jane arrived for dinner instead of Sam. Sam had called earlier, excited about being invited out to a basketball game with a coworker. She knew how much he loved the sport, so she told him it was no problem and called Jane at work immediately. She arrived at 6 pm with dessert in hand.

"Okay, what can I do?" she asked after placing the cake in the fridge.

"Nothing. Just help yourself to something to drink," Emily said as waited for the oil to heat up in her frying pan.

Jane poured herself some water and watched as Emily started to stir fry dinner.

"I'm making your favourite," she said as she cooked the green beans.

"Hmm...smells sooo good!" Jane smiled. "So, what's new? How are things going with your mom?"

"Actually, not bad."

"Really?"

"Yeah. She seems to be responding to Dr. Lee's treatment and, catch this," Emily paused and turned her full attention to Jane. "She actually wants to go on a cruise with my aunt!"

"Wow, are you serious?" Jane asked.

Emily nodded her head excitedly.

"That's great news! She must be feeling good!"

"Yeah, I just saw her today at the clinic. She looks stronger, healthier now. Dr. Lee seemed happy with her progress too." Emily felt surprised by the conviction in her voice.

"Hmm, that is unbelievable! I'm so happy for you!" Jane gave her a hug.

"Thanks...thanks," she said. "But..."

"Yes, but..."

Emily explained how Sam's cousin had given them a name of a specialist to see, but the GP wouldn't make a referral.

"I'm sorry Emily," she said.

"Yeah and I thought maybe about asking my aunt for help but Auntie Sue doesn't think it's necessary to see anyone else," Emily heard herself say. Ma's smiling and pouting face went through her mind. "I don't want to upset Ma either with more treatment, you know?"

Jane nodded. "I think it can be so hard on the patient and family," she said. Jane relayed a story she just heard from her cousin about some distant relative undergoing cancer treatment. "Side effects can be brutal, like sickness, pain, fatigue and losing your hair."

"Yes and that's the part I don't know that Ma could take! Especially losing her hair – she's so proud of her good black hair!"

Jane nodded and continued about how the family has to take this relative to treatment, support him through it and pretend that he's looking better. "I mean maybe he's getting better because they're killing the cancer, but boy, you go through a lot of suffering first."

Emily listened as she finished cooking. *Ma couldn't handle this kind of treatment!* She served the rice and stir fry onto two plates. *I can't handle it either.* Jane took the plates to the table and they sat down to eat.

"I don't think my mother will go through it," she said with some conviction.

"Then forget about it," said Jane.

"Dig in," she said feeling somewhat better about her decision.

Jane started to eat. "Mmm, this is so good!"

"Thanks," she said as she started to eat. "So, what is going on with you?"

"Same old, you know?"

"Still knee-deep in research?"

Jane laughed and told her about some of the stuff she had been researching and trying to link to her thesis.

"Want some more?" she asked as Jane finished her plate.

"Maybe a tiny bit more. I'll help myself," she said getting up. "You want some?"

"Sure, you can load me up for a small second too. I'll get us some more water." She took the Brita from the fridge and filled their glasses. Jane brought their plates back and they started to eat again. She thought about Auntie Sue's reaction to Sam.

"Jane?"

"Umhum?"

"What do you think of Sam meeting my mother right now? I told my aunt about him..."

"What?!" Jane shouted excitedly. "Really? I've been wanting you to do this all along!"

"Really?" Emily felt confused.

"Well, you know I get it, and I don't get why you hide this stuff from your mother," said Jane.

Emily was stunned. Jane had never said that before.

"I mean, sure, I don't have to introduce every Tom, Dick and Harry to my parents, but a boyfriend...well that's different."

"Sure, it's easy with parents like yours," Emily pouted. Jane always seemed to have it so easy! Easy time meeting men; easy time talking to her parents. No one was criticizing her!

"Well..." Jane paused and studied her.

"What?" she asked straightening her posture.

"It's just that Sam is important to you, right?"

"Yes..."

"Maybe it won't be so bad?" She tried. "Maybe your mom will like him?"

"But Jane, you know about the fights..."

"Yes, but if not now, then when?"

She loved and hated this pushy side of Jane. *Dammit! What if she is right? What if Ma never meets him?* Fear and anger took hold of her and visions of crying and shouting at her mother filled her mind. "I...I just don't know," she finally said.

"Give it some time. I'll help you, really, I will," Jane said supportively.

She looked at Jane's beautiful blue eyes and blonde hair. *If only...*she thought wistfully. Jane had two younger siblings and both her parents were professionals. Her dad was a lawyer and mom was a teacher. Jane claimed that her mom was her "best friend" and Emily was quite shocked to find her talking on the phone with her for hours about her problems, like she was talking to someone like her. *How can this be?* Emily didn't get it, and she'd question her about what her mom said or how she reacted.

"You didn't tell her about that fling, did you?" Emily asked one time.

"Of course not!" Jane said annoyed. "Why would I bother her about things that don't matter?"

Emily was secretly pleased that Jane kept secrets from her mom, like her. Later, in second year university, Jane had a pregnancy scare and Emily was totally floored when her mom showed up at the doctor's office on campus. Jane crumbled into her mother's arms and she just held her. After it was determined that she wasn't pregnant, Emily was certain that a big speech about safe sex was coming. She waited to hear about it, but instead Jane's mother took her, Jane and Jane's boyfriend Tom out to dinner. After she left, Emily probed Jane for the lecture. She was sure her mother had said something!

"Be careful," said Jane. "That's what my mom said."

"That's it?" Emily was stunned. She could hear her own mother going on about what a bad man Tom was, and how they shouldn't be having sex, and what if people found out, and good girls don't do these things. It would have been insufferable! She was so envious of Jane because she had White, professional parents who accepted and forgave her. These things don't happen in Chinese families – at least not ones with newly immigrated parents like Emily knew.

"You are so lucky," she finally said to Jane, who smiled and nodded.

"I know. That's why she's like my best friend."

"Let's have something chocolate..." Jane said at the dinner table

"That'll make us feel better!" Jane sprang from her seat and took the chocolate cake from the fridge. "Just what the doctor ordered!" she joked as she returned with two dessert plates.

Emily took a bite of the cake. She smiled at Jane and said, "Mmm..." Her friend smiled back. She continued to eat, letting the bitterness of the chocolate fill her mouth.

After Jane left, Emily decided to have a bath. She poured some lavender bubble bath into the rapidly filling tub before walking back to the kitchen to put the leftover food into the fridge. She checked the kitchen and the dining room; everything looked neat and tidy thanks to Jane. The water continued to thunder out as she took her white bathrobe from the back of the bedroom door, returned to the bathroom and turned the water off. Reaching down, she winced as she quickly withdrew her hand from the hot water. She decided to wash her face and brush her teeth to give the water time to cool off. After this she tested the water again, before undressing. As she placed one foot in, she heard the phone ring. She ran out to grab the cordless phone from her bedroom.

"Hello?" she said as she descended into the white foam.

"Hey you," said Sam.

"Hi! How was the game?" She was happy to hear Sam's voice.

"Good." Sam told her about the basketball game, what they ate and how many beers they drank.

"Three beers! That's quite a bit for you, isn't it?"

"Nah," he said laughing. "I can handle three beers – I don't usually drink as much with you, that's all. How about you? Did you have a nice time with Jane?"

"Yeah," she replied and told him about most of their evening. She left out the part about him meeting her mother.

"Well, guess I'd better go and get ready for bed," Sam said.

"Yeah..." she said and paused. *Should I?* Impulsively she added, "Sam, can I ask you something?"

"Sure."

"Um...I've been thinking about introducing you to my mom."

"Really?"

"Yes. Would you like that?"

"Of course, Emily! I've been asking you about that for a while."

"Yeah, I know," she said slowly.

"What made you change your mind?"

"Oh, I kinda mentioned you to my Auntie Sue..." She didn't bother to go into the details of what Jane said.

"You did?"

"Well, I had to explain about how I got the other specialist, right?"

"Uh huh...and? Hey, what did you decide about that specialist anyway?"

"Well, I spoke with Auntie Sue and we decided against it for now."

"Really? Are you sure?" Sam seemed surprised.

"Well, yeah, I mean Ma is getting stronger and Jane was telling me how horrible cancer treatment is. I can't imagine my mom doing well there, you know?"

"I guess so."

You guess so? Emily shoved the bubbles in her bath away from her. "I'm doing my best, you know Sam!"

Sam tried to make amends, "I know, I know you are! You know what's best, Em. I'm so happy you decided to let me meet your mother!" he added.

149

Did I? Suddenly, she felt exhausted. "I'm tired," she finally said after a few minutes of silence. "Can we talk about this tomorrow?"

"Yeah, I think that's a good idea. Get some sleep, Sweetie," and he made a kissing sound into the phone.

"Yeah, goodnight," she said and clicked the phone off. She closed her eyes and tried to shake away that sour image of her mother's face.

Chapter Twelve

Three days came and went. Emily found herself immersed in work: typing reports and doing assessments. When she got home Thursday at noon, she went to the kitchen and heated up a can of mushroom soup. Then she took out the brown bread and made herself a sandwich with Mortadella, honey mustard, lettuce, tomato and some processed cheese. Seating herself at the dining room table, she took a bite of her sandwich and stirred the beige-coloured soup to cool it down. Every night since Monday, she and Sam talked briefly about how he should meet her mother. Emily kept envisioning some lovely evening ending in a shouting match between herself and her mother. As Sam spoke, pressure seemed to mount in her head, growing until she found herself blowing up like a steaming kettle. "That's not a good idea, Sam," she would shout or "I don't know! That's enough for now, okay?" Initially Sam remained calm. Last night he got upset.

"Look Emily, I'm getting tired of this!" he said. "You don't like anything I suggest, so why don't you decide how we should do this and tell me?"

"But I do want your input Sam," she said trying to sound encouraging.

"Really? I don't think you do because whatever I suggest is a bad idea to you and you know what? I'm getting tired of this, and I have no more things to suggest right now. In fact, we can even forget about it if you want!"

She felt like she had been slapped in the face. *He doesn't want to meet my mother?* At first she felt insulted, followed by a feeling of relief. *Maybe we don't have to do this?*

"Look Emily, let's just call it a night, okay?" Sam said coldly.

"Okay," she said as the phone went dead. She hung up and walked out of her bedroom and into the living room. She paced about tidying up her apartment, wiping at her eyes and trying to imagine a smile on her mother's face when she introduced Sam to her. *Why do we even have to do this?* Her life had been so much simpler before. She and Sam used to carry on the way they pleased. They'd go out, take weekend trips, be seen in public without her ever worrying about being caught. Hadn't she moved to Toronto to get away from her mom's influence? Emily sighed. She couldn't see how this could end happily.

Back when she was a child, maybe around age six, she vividly remembered her mother coming up to her and sweetly asking, "Emily-a. You marry Chinese? Make your mama happy?" What can a six-year-old do, but answer "yes." Even then, she felt the lie in her heart, when she heard her response. It was required of her to obey her mother. She heard it time and time again growing up.

During the teenage dating years, she relished in her rebellion dating whatever ethnicity she pleased. It was easy when she didn't have a serious boyfriend. Not that Emily didn't want one; it just never worked out. Sure, she had one relationship lasting a year during her final grade of high school with Steven, but it seemed more like a friendship with spurts of physical contact here and there. She liked the convenience of having a date for all the important school events and everyone at school referred to them as "an item." Emily worked most weekends at her dad's restaurant, so Steve was free to party on his own. At the end of high school, they parted ways amicably, and she was happy to start anew at university. Her promise to her mom never even entered her mind until she met Rory during frosh week.

Rory looked like a high school dreamboat, with his wavy dirty blonde hair, chiseled features and athletic build. Anyone who set eyes on him expected him to be a jock. He wasn't. He liked sports, but he was very serious about his studies and was set on becoming a physicist. Emily was drawn to him physically and mentally. For the first time, she met someone she wanted a serious relationship with. They dated

153

exclusively and she referred to him as her "boyfriend". He didn't object to the title, although she wasn't sure he reciprocated it. Everything felt so right with Rory and she let him be the first to have her. It wasn't as magical as she had expected, but after the first love making, it got easier and became a regular part of their time together. She began to dream of their life together and, strangely enough thoughts, of Rory meeting her parents began to creep into her mind. Rory wasn't interested in meeting them and never even brought the subject up. Still, fears of being caught permeated her thoughts and she instructed him over and over again to not come over when her parents were around. Maybe he got tired of her neurotic behaviour because he suggested they take a break to date other people when school ended. Emily was devastated and blamed the breakup on her parents. It was because of them he dumped her! Of course, she knew the truth was that she was acting like an idiot. During their last month together, she had been irritable, irrational and picked fights with him for no particular reason. Well, there was a reason or maybe there were many reasons, but she didn't want to admit to herself or to anyone else that her mother could drive her to act so crazy. She convinced herself she'd handle it better in the future.

"So, how am I doing?" Emily wondered out loud, now seated in front of the computer. She tried to reassure herself, but still the uncertainty remained. *How is this situation different? Wasn't she acting crazy again?* After Rory, she decided she wouldn't allow her parents in her life until she was engaged or had eloped or something. *That way there would be nothing to argue about.* Her mother's illness has changed everything! Her fingers pounded as she tried to work through the document. Of course, she had occasional thoughts about Sam meeting her mother before all this sickness stuff came up, but she always managed to stuff it away. She had even been successful at putting Sam off from meeting her with statements like, "Oh, her English isn't so good," or "She doesn't like Canadian food," or "She just likes to play Mahjong." *Now what to do?* Emily closed her report up. She wished she could stop all of this. She shuffled her files around and sighed. She knew she had to do what she dreaded.

Friday afternoon, Emily found herself pulling into her mother's driveway. *Home again.* As much as she wanted to avoid discussing this Sam situation with her mom, she couldn't shake it from her mind. She took the heavy bag of oranges from the trunk and walked to the porch. She had her house key ready and let herself in. It was almost four o'clock.

"Hello?" she called out as she closed the door behind her shut.

"Emily?" called Auntie Sue who emerged from the kitchen. "Good timing. Your Ma just got up from a nap. She's in the bathroom," she said looking up at Ma's opened bedroom door.

She nodded and followed Auntie Sue back into the kitchen. As usual, a big stainless steel soup pot was cooking on the stove.

"What kind of soup are you making?" she asked.

"White fungus," Auntie Sue replied as she opened the soup lid, letting steam escape to the humming fan. "Do you want some?"

She nodded as she took a seat at the head of the brown kitchen table and ran her finger along the familiar pattern.

"Be ready soon. Are you staying for supper?"

"Sure," she said looking up. "I have no plans."

"No plans? How come?" her aunt asked as she took a seat to her right.

"No reason. Why?" she asked with chuckle.

"Did something happen between you and that goi-law?" she asked in a hushed tone.

"No! Why?" She asked as her ears tingled.

"Then when are you going to introduce him to your mother?"

"Well, we are talking about it..." she said slowly.

"Uh huh."

"I don't know. Maybe I should talk to her about this during dinner?"

"Yes, yes!" Auntie Sue said excitedly. "This is a good idea. Don't worry. I will help you, okay?" she said as she touched Emily's arm.

"Oh...okay," she said as her stomach tightened. *Will she really help?*

Ma appeared and seemed quite pleased to see her. She tried to take over cooking dinner and argued happily with her sister about how to prepare the meal. "Emily likes the vegetables crunchy!" she advised.

"But we old people have no teeth and need to eat soft vegetables," her aunt argued. "I'll just take some out for her early, okay?"

Ma nodded.

Emily laughed and added, "Don't worry! I don't mind soft vegetables, really!"

Ma and Auntie Sue looked at each other and started laughing even more. She didn't think her comment was that funny, but tried to laugh along to fit in. When dinner was ready, the three women sat down to eat. Emily stayed at the head of the table, Ma sat to her right and Auntie Sue went around the table to sit at to her left. They began eating.

"How is Uncle Henry?" she asked.

"Oh he is fine. I went by yesterday and cook him some food. He can eat the same thing for two or three days, he doesn't care."

"Poor Uncle!"

"Emily is right. You should ask him to join us for supper!"

"Sure, but he doesn't care, really."

"Less work for you. You working too hard!" Ma said sternly.

"Yeah, Ma's right. Why cook at two places?" Emily asked.

Then Ma added, "Little sister, I take up too much of your time. Why don't go home? I feel much better. You help me too much! Now I heat up food and can cook myself. I am stronger."

Emily and her aunt stared at Ma.

"You no longer want my help?" Auntie Sue said.

"No, no, no," Ma said shaking her head in disagreement. "Thanks for help, but you have husband at home, and I take you away from him."

"Ma, maybe you should let Auntie Sue keep helping you a bit longer," Emily tried feeling worried.

"Yes and how will you get to your appointments with Dr. Lee?" Auntie Sue challenged.

"Please, don't be angry, Sue. Yes, I like you take me to appointments, but also go home to husband, okay?"

Both women said nothing, but continued to eat. Emily looked at her aunt and at her mother. *Why's Ma pushing Auntie Sue to go home? Is she really better?* An awkward rift seemed to have formed between the two women. She was unaccustomed to being the negotiator. Wasn't it usually her and Ma at odds? *What would Dad do here to mend the problem?* She knew. She'd seen Dad do it a million times. She'd bring up Sam to change the subject and all would be forgotten. *Is this really the best time?* Her mother did seem to be in a good mood. She took a breath, looked straight ahead and blurted out, "Ma, I have a boyfriend. He is a goi-law. Don't be mad." She slowly turned to face her mother. Ma was looking down at her rice bowl, her lips posed in that pout. *She's mad.* She turned to her aunt, paralyzed.

Auntie Sue jumped right in. "Ah...Emily, hmm, is he a good person?"

"Yes, a very good person." She was thankful for her help.

"Oh and does he have a good job?"

"Yes, he is an accountant."

"Wow, you see Big Sister, your daughter has found a good match. Accountants make good money." Auntie Sue winked at her.

Ma looked up. Her arms were folded across her chest, her pout now reduced to a sneer. She sighed long and loud, "Ai, what can I do?" She shook her head.

"We should meet him!" Auntie Sue said decidedly. "Yes, let's meet him for dinner."

Can we just forget the whole thing? Emily nodded uneasily back. She glared at her mother's sullen face. *Why can't she be happy for me?* She really regretted bringing the whole idea up, but did she have any choice? Meanwhile, Auntie Sue was continuing her sales pitch to Ma.

"Does he use chopsticks?" She grinned wildly.

Emily stopped herself from rolling her eyes. *Auntie Sue was trying.* "Yes!" she said with false enthusiasm. "He does and he loves Chinese food!"

"This goi-law is good," Auntie Sue said to her mother. "Why don't we have dinner with him tomorrow night?"

Ma didn't respond, so Auntie Sue and Emily decided upon Sunday. After that Emily gulped through her dinner, barely bringing her head up for air. She blurted some excuse about work afterwards and ran to her car. Everything had gone as well as possible, but she felt uneasy, sick. As she headed out of town, she recalled that awful teenaged fight she had with Ma about George, the boy on her porch who wasn't even her boyfriend. After the breakup phone call, Ma confronted her. She told her that the goi-law was "no good" and "bad" and that a "marriage with a goi-law would end in divorce." Emily already felt devastated, but her mother's words ate at her broken heart. *Could she be right? No!* She refused to believe it and she started to scream back, the way any angry teenager fights back. Hurtful, disrespectful words flew from her mouth, as she accused her mom of being "an ignorant peasant who knew nothing about love." Ma called her a "bad girl" and sulked away. She felt victorious, but wasn't sure what she had won. She had that same sick feeling now.

"This is going to be just great," she said out loud mockingly to break her mind trip and attend to driving. She jacked up the radio to block out her thoughts and sang along until she reached home.

Chapter Thirteen

After her shower Saturday morning, Emily dressed and waited for Sam to arrive. Last night's conversation with her mother and aunt was still fresh in her mind. She forced herself to sit on the couch and relax. Sam arrived looking fresh and inviting in his light blue cotton shirt and blue jeans. She embraced him, feeling at ease in his arms. *It'll be okay.*

"You look nice," she said smiling. "I missed you."

"I missed you too," he said as they kissed. They held hands and walked arm and arm down the street together towards the local diner for breakfast. Inside, they took a seat in a booth and opened the menu.

"Hungry?" he asked.

"Sort of...what are you going to have?"

"Probably some poached eggs and bacon."

"The usual, you mean?" she said laughing. Sam had introduced poached eggs to her, and she had incorporated it into her breakfast ritual with Jane. "Maybe I'll have poached eggs too, but with some sausages."

"Sounds good," he said as their coffees arrived. They ordered and chatted about the workweek. When their breakfast arrived, Emily took a bite of her eggs and looked at Sam who was busy pouring ketchup onto his plate. *He's so nice. How can she not like him?*

"So, I saw my mother yesterday." Emily began.

"Oh?"

"Yeah and well, I mentioned you." She felt that lump in her throat return.

Sam put the ketchup bottle down and looked at her. "Really?"

She nodded.

"So, what did she say? Or what did you say about me?" he asked excitedly.

"Nothing much. I just told her that I had a White boyfriend and that he was an accountant."

He laughed and added, "Yeah, a bean counter, but not a boring one!"

She smiled.

"So? Was she upset? Does your mother want to meet me?"

"Yes...well, sort of," she said in between bites. "My aunt and I arranged for the four of us to have dinner tomorrow night, if you're free."

Sam looked stunned. "Really?"

"Yeah. Are you...I mean do you want to have dinner tomorrow?" Her heart raced.

"Of course!" he replied excitedly. "Are you okay with this?"

"I think so..."

Sam stared at her and waited.

"Well...I'm not sure, but I guess there's no easy way to do this either," she stammered.

He nodded.

"But we are going to my mother's favourite Chinese restaurant, and that always puts her in a good mood," she said fervently. She told him about the restaurant and watched Sam's face brighten.

"Okay," he said, "I'm ready for this! Don't worry, it's going to work out, Em, I'm sure of it!"

She smiled and agreed with him, but felt the butterflies churn in her stomach. *Is this really going to work?* Ma didn't say anything after Sam was introduced to the dinner conversation. *What if she sulks all through dinner?*

"Em?" Sam said, bringing her back to their conversation.

"I'm sorry, what did you say?"

"What do I call your mother in Chinese?"

"Oh," she said, "That. It's not really necessary, Sam." *Why are we talking about this again?*

"Sweetie," he said reaching for her hand. "I want to try to impress her. Maybe she'll like me, who knows right?"

"Is this really important? Trying to say Chinese words to her?" Emily's fist clenched as that childhood taunt went through her head.

"Yes, yes, I think it is important," said Sam as he reached across the table for her hand.

She didn't want to tell him. She sat back, out of reach and looked at his pleading face. *Why should I?*

"Come on, Sweetie," he tried. "I think it'll help her to like me."

She rubbed at her head. *He seems so sincere.* "Promise you won't laugh at my Chinese?"

Sam put his hand on his heart. "I swear it."

She stared at his wide opened eyes. *He means it?*

Sam moved forward to caress her face. "I won't laugh."

She pulled away again and exhaled. "Okay, just say jeu siem or siem," she said, cringing as she spoke.

"Jew seem," tried Sam.

"Sure, sure, good enough."

Let me try again. "Jew siem..."

"That's fine, fine," said Emily cutting Sam off. She peered down at her remaining poached egg. White and glossy, yellow contents hidden. As a child, she learned how to speak Chinese first and English second. Ma always spoke to her in Chinese, even outside in front of other kids. No one said anything, until one day when this kid was visiting his grandparents in the neighbourhood. He started to laugh when he heard her speaking Chinese and teased her with that Chinese, Japanese taunt. She was mortified. *What did he mean?* She felt ashamed even though she didn't know why. She avoided speaking Chinese after that. Ma scolded her calling her "Jok-Sing." Did Ma have it right? Maybe she wasn't yellow on the outside, but white. She clenched at her fork and thrust it through the remaining egg. Yellow contents bled out, covering the remaining whites.

"Emily?"

She looked up at Sam who had still been practicing his Chinese. "You're doing fine," she said and stuffed some egg into her mouth.

Later that day, they found themselves on Bloor Street, walking and browsing in the boutiques and high-end retail stores. Yorkville, as the area was known, was filled with expensive shops, restaurants and designer stores. It is bounded by Bloor Street to the south, Davenport Road to the north, Yonge Street to the east and Avenue Road to the west. It is a former village and home to the hippie movement in the

1960s. It transitioned into a shopping area after the Bloor-Danforth subway was constructed. Emily loved the retailer Holt Renfrew for its selection of international and Canadian designers. She loved to browse here; buying wasn't usually an option, and the snobby salespeople never made her feel welcomed either. She admired the brightly coloured spring fashions and touched the soft cottons, silks and nylon blends. Shopping was a great distraction.

"Try something on, Em," Sam said.

"Nah," she said and shook her head, "nothing on sale," she mouthed to him. She only shopped sales.

""So what? I'd like to buy you something." Sam picked up a pink sweater. "This would look nice on you."

Pink. Ma's colour. She pushed it down. "Um...I'm not crazy about pink."

"Okay," he said. "You choose."

She took a baby blue one and held it up against her.

"That looks nice. Try it on."

Emily searched for the price tag. $99.50. Regular price. "Kinda pricey, right now." She folded the sweater and placed it on the pile.

"Really?" Sam grabbed the sweater and looked at the price tag. "This isn't bad. Here." He handed her the blue top again. "Try it on. Come on, for me."

"But Sam," she said, "it's not on sale."

"So what?"

She bore into his smiling face. *He really wants me to try this.* "Okay," she said surprised and took the garment into the ladies change room. Inside the cubicle, she took her brown t-shirt off and pulled the V-neck on. She stared into the narrow full- length mirror. Her face seemed brighter, and the shoulders felt comfortable in the soft blue cotton. She smiled and grabbed at the price tag on the sleeve. *Later. It'll go on sale soon.* She changed and came out.

"Hey, where's the top?" Sam asked.

"It's okay, Hon," she said dropping the top into a colourful heap.

"Sure?"

She smiled and took his hand, making a mental note to check the price in a few week's time.

"Do you mind if we look for some men's shoes?" he asked.

"Sure," she said as they descended the escalator.

In the shoe department, Sam inspected different options, until he settled on a pair of black loafers. "What do you think?" he asked.

"Not bad. How much?" She felt apprehensive.

"About two hundred dollars," he said as he took a seat to try the shoes on.

She sat down and watched as Sam walked around to test out the shoes.

"They feel pretty good," he said.

She nodded and picked up a similar pair in a tan colour. "Is the price good?" she whispered to him as she looked at the price tag on the bottom of the shoe.

"I think so," he said as he sat down to put on his old shoes. "Besides, I really need a new pair right now."

"We could check out some other stores to compare, if you like," she pressed.

"Nah. I think these are okay," he said and got up and to pay for the new shoes.

"Come on Sam!" she tried to grab his hand. "We've still got time to look around!"

"It's no big deal, Em, really," he said ignoring her, while he handed his Visa card to a sales person.

Emily marched over to the shoe racks. Compulsively she picked up shoe after shoe, determined to find a pair on sale.

"What are you doing?" Sam asked as he approached her with his new sales bag in hand.

"Hold on," she said as she grabbed a couple more shoe styles. "Nothing's on sale!" she said frustrated, giving up the hunt.

Sam looked bewildered. "Em, I told you, these are fine."

"Okay, fine, if you don't need my help, just say so," she barked and stormed over to the escalators up. *Crazy goi-law, she heard in her head.*

"What's the big deal?" Sam asked, racing up to her.

"Nothing," she snapped looking straight ahead. She was seething but didn't know why. *What am I doing?* She felt like she wanted to scream and shout at Sam. *Why?*

"Okay, so can we just forget about this?" Sam suggested.

"Sure, let's drop it" she growled with slithered eyes. Her anger raged, threatening to consume them both. She got off the escalator and stomped into the ladies shoe section on the second floor. Barely noticing the shoe she had she stuffed her foot in and modeled it in front of the mirror. Sam sat down and waited.

Emily checked the sales price. *Yep, FULL PRICE.* Ma wouldn't approve as she never bought anything that wasn't on sale. It never crossed Emily's mind to either. *Why waste the money?* "Unlike you Sam, I can't afford to buy these right now!" she said and put the shoes away. Sam didn't respond, but looked wounded. Her eyes instantly welled up

171

when their eyes locked and she turned away ashamed. She was like a child again being berated by her mother, only Sam was the child! *Who was she? Ma?*

She left abruptly, leaving Sam behind. *God, what am I| doing?* Outside, the sun continued to shine and the air was warm and mild even though it was almost six o'clock. She steadied herself against a concrete planter that held a tree, newly exploding with greenness. Emily breathed in the freshness until her nausea disappeared. Sam appeared and waited.

"Where do you want to go next?" he asked quietly.

Relieved, she grabbed his hand and held it tight. She wanted to apologize. "I'm sorry, Sam," played in her head, but she said nothing, fearful it would come out wrong. Instead, she brought his coupled hand to her heart and prayed that he understood. They moved down the street this way, until she believed her message had been received and he had forgiven her.

At Pho Happiness Restaurant, they ordered a rare beef pho, vermicelli with chicken and a spring roll and some salad rolls. The crowd and noise at this popular university hang out shifted their attention to their appetites. She picked up the freshly wrapped rice paper rolls, feeling its cool texture and sniffed at the basil, shrimp and pork to ensure they were fresh.

"Yum..." she said as she plunged the roll into peanut sauce before taking a bite.

"Good?"

She nodded. Eating always put her at ease and Emily ate eagerly. "I'm really hungry!" she said.

"Yeah, me too," Sam said as he took a bite of his salad roll.

The waitress came up to their table with a tray and placed the large steaming bowl of soup in front of Sam and the other bowl in front of Emily.

"Hot sauce, please," she said to the waitress, before emptying the dish of fish sauce into the vermicelli bowl. She picked up her chopsticks and removed the spring roll before mixing the noodles, chicken and peanuts up.

Sam squeezed fresh lime into the soup after adding the sprouts and basil. "Nice," he said as he tasted the broth.

A bottle of chili sauce was placed on their table and Sam put a dab of it into the hoisin sauce to dip his beef in. They ate in silent content.

"Want some?" she asked when her bowl was over half empty.

"Sure," he said and they switched bowls. "So what do you want to do tonight?"

"Don't know. You?"

"We could go catch a show?"

"Can we make the early show?"

"Probably," he said as he looked at his watch. "It's only 6:45."

"Or we could go home and pick up a movie?" she suggested. She put her chopsticks down beside the empty soup bowl.

"That's okay too."

"Let's just check out what is playing and if there isn't anything to see, go home?" he said.

They agreed, finished dinner and got up leave. She went towards the washroom, as Sam stopped at the cashier to pay the bill.

"Hey, isn't it my treat?" she said, walking back.

"No, don't worry about it."

"But you paid for breakfast this morning," she said as she pulled out her wallet.

"I got it," Sam said as the cashier gave him the bill to sign. "Go to the washroom, already!"

"Okay," she said putting her Visa away. "But I pay for the movie!" she said as she raced to the toilets.

Outside they headed east back across Bloor Street and cut through an alleyway that led to the movie theatres. They looked at their choices: *The Fifth Element* or *Father's Day*.

"Hmm," Emily said. "Anything interest you?"

"Maybe *The Fifth Element*?"

"Or *Father's Day* at 7:30?"

"I'm not sure if I'm in the mood for a chick flick," he teased.

"Chick flick? What's that supposed to mean?" she asked testily.

"I'm just kidding! Of course, that looks like a good choice too."

"But you think *The Fifth Element* would be more interesting?" she demanded.

"Just more entertaining, that's all." He tried more softly. "Come on, you want to see *Father's Day*, so let's get tickets." He pulled her by the arm to ticket booth. "Two for *Father's Day*," he said as he reached for his wallet.

"I got it!" Emily snapped. "I told you earlier, it's my turn!"

"Okay, okay," Sam said and stepped out of the way.

She yanked $20 from her green leather wallet and gave it to the cashier. Two tickets were printed out, which she grabbed as she moved towards the usher.

"Enjoy the show," he said as he handed her back the ticket stubs.

She had already lost interest in the movie, but the smell of popcorn distracted her and led her to the shortest food line up. Sam hustled to keep up with her.

"You want me to go get our seats?" he asked.

"Can't you wait?"

"I have to go to the washroom now, so I could do that and then get our seats."

"Okay, but where are you going to sit?"

"I'll find some good seats in the middle," he said as he took his ticket from her and walked away. "I'll keep an eye out for you," he said.

"Sam, what do you want to eat?" she called after him. Her mood had soured again and she started to feel edgy. *Should I forget the popcorn?*

He turned around and said, "Just some of your drink."

She watched until he disappeared into the men's room. The couple in front of her had finished paying. *Good. It'll be quick.* She glanced again at the men's washroom door. *Maybe I'll get our stuff before Sam gets out.*

"Can I help you?" the server said.

"Oh," Emily said surprised. She looked at the menu and ordered a large ice tea and small popcorn.

"Do you want butter?"

"No, thanks," she said. While she waited, she stared hard in the direction of the men's washroom. *Where is that guy?* She paid, took the food and ran towards the restrooms. She had seen a couple of guys leave the washroom while she was waiting for food, but neither of them were Sam. She looked at her watch. It was 7:23. Come on, come on, she muttered as she paced outside the door. Just then the door opened and someone came out.

"Uh, excuse me," she said as she rushed at the blonde-haired guy.

He paused, startled, and looked at her. "Yes?" he blurted.

"I'm waiting for my boyfriend and a..."

"I was the only one in there," he said as he walked around her.

"You sure?" she demanded.

"Sorry," he said as he moved quickly to the theatres.

Damn! I missed him! Agitation was building. She searched her left and right jean pocket. *Whew, I've got it.* She pulled out the movie ticket, raced to the theatres. She chose the left entrance, hoping there would be less people seated. *Please let there be lights,* she prayed as she walked slowly in. The available lights flickered from the trailers on the large movie screen. She blinked and blinked. *God, why am I so blind? Damned these contacts!* She cursed as she squinted, staring up at a sea of blank faces.

"Sam?" she called out in a child-like whisper. Her heart pounded wildly as she frantically scanned the aisles from left to right, then from right to left. Suddenly the audience erupted into laughter. *Are they laughing at me?* Her cheeks flushed and she felt like she was lost, unable to see, like she was in Grade 1, before she got eyeglasses. Something salty touched the corner of her mouth and she spun around. *Damn!* She forced her shaking legs back out of the theatre. When she got to the hallway, she stopped and waited for her eyes to focus. She wiped her tears away and rubbed her ringing ears. *God, that was stupid!* She swore out loud.

"Emily!"

She looked over her shoulder and saw Sam. Her fury grew. *Why didn't he help me?*

He came running up to her. "Where are you going?" he asked. "I called you, stood up and waved at you, but you kept walking!"

"I couldn't find you, so I thought you'd left!" she accused.

"Left? Why would I leave? Have you been crying?" he said looking at her face. She moved further from him. *Was he being honest?* Her head spun.

"What's going on? What's wrong?" Sam appeared baffled.

"I don't know..." she stammered. "Why didn't you just wait for me, like I had asked?" she demanded.

"I'm sorry," he said as he tried to pull her near. "Okay, what do you want to do? The movie hasn't started yet. We can still catch it."

"You don't want to watch this 'chick flick' anyways," she grumbled.

"Em, come on! I said I was sorry," he said exasperated.

She saw Sam's furrowed brow and grimaced mouth. At the same time, Ma's pouted face flashed through her mind. *Maybe she's right? Maybe we won't work out?*

Fearful of what was coming next, she took flight. "Look, I can't stay," she blurted as she hurried out, tossing the popcorn and drink away.

"Going? Where are you going?" Sam appealed.

"Home!" She shot back with red eyes. Scared like a child running from a horror film, she took off down the street ignoring Sam's calls. *What am I afraid of?* By the time she got to Yonge Street, out of breath and sweating heavily, she really didn't know what she was running from. She hunched down to catch her breath in front of the subway doors. *Where was Sam?* Her anger had been drained away and she felt stupid and alone. *God, I'm such a loser!* Had somebody taunted her? She didn't know, but a feeling of being ridiculed and laughed at overcame her. *Crazy girl!* She heard Ma's voice scream out. Maybe she was crazy. Could someone like Sam really love her? *Sam.* She turned around scanned for his familiar shape in the bodies down the street. He wasn't there. She'd really done it now. Defeated, she rode the subway back to the apartment.

Chapter Fourteen

When she opened her eyes next, she found light in her room with the sun shining between the slats of the vertical blinds. *Sam?* She reached beside her, but knew that no one was there. Abandoned. All last night, she listened for his footsteps to arrive at her door, eventually falling into a fitful sleep. Her whole body ached as she made her way to the washroom to shower and get ready for the day. It was nine o'clock when she sat down at the dining room table with a bowl of cereal and a cup of coffee. Ahead of her, on the bookcase was her telephone. She stared at the phone as she crunched on the dry Mini Wheats cereal and drummed her free hand on the brown box. *Have I lost him? This is Ma's fault!* She pushed the cereal box away and busied herself cleaning up the dishes.

To occupy herself, Emily turned to the menial task of doing laundry. She went into the bedroom to strip the bed and sorted the laundry from the wicker hamper into two piles: darks and lights. The blue plastic laundry basket was stored on the top shelf of the hallway closet, which she could reach if she stood on the tips of her toes. She pulled it down, placed the pile of light-coloured clothes into it and went downstairs to the laundry room with her empty film container of quarters. The lock of the door was a bit sticky and she fidgeted with the key until it opened. Inside, the two washing machines and dryers were empty since it was still early – only 9:30 – so she threw in the clothes and detergent, started up the machine and ran back upstairs to grab the other load. She raced back down to the basement, relieved to find the second washing machine still empty and started up the dark load. Both machines were rumbling and clanking before she left the laundry room.

Back in her apartment, she went into the office and turned the computer on. She sat at her desk, grabbed the top file folder from the plastic tray at the top right corner of her desk and opened it up. After each assessment, she would place the client's file on the bottom of her in tray so that she could complete them in the order she had seen them. *Hmm...Mr. Terry Brown* and she reviewed the information she had gathered on him from their meeting on Monday. She began by filling in the general information box she had created and used for the front page of her report, then stared blankly at the screen. Sam's face dashed through her mind. *Things were good until Ma got in the way!* She pounded her fists into the keyboard and her eyes blurred with tears. *Oh God! Did I lose him?* She stared at the motionless phone beside her. *Call Sam? What if he's mad?* Fear of Sam's reaction paralyzed her. Instead, she switched her attention back to the computer and started typing. She wrote quickly for about an hour and was almost at the end of the report when she remembered her laundry.

Dashing downstairs with quarters in one hand and dryer sheets in the other, she opened the laundry room to find both washers in use and her clean wet laundry sitting in the empty dryers. *Dammit!* She hated it when strangers touched her things and rammed the machine on. She was already annoyed, when her right knee started to crack as she climbed the stairs.

"Old age, Em," Sam had joked when he heard the cracking sound. *Sam...*he was on her mind again, worsening her foul mood! She stomped across the hall and yanked open the apartment door. Inside, she sat back down at her computer and looked at her watch. It was eleven o'clock. *Should I call?* Even though she knew she should pick up the phone, she couldn't bring herself to and continued to type lackadaisically.

Not since Rory, had she felt so right with someone, and she really hadn't expected to fall in love with Sam. Rory was always the type of guy she thought she'd love. Serious, smart, insightful, they could have philosophical discussions about almost anything! Their conversations were verbose and thrilling, if they shared the same opinion. She discovered how opinionated and arrogant he could be, hating him at times as much as she loved him. He acted like he was committed to their relationship, even told her he loved her. One day, he shared his fantasy about this other woman and she flipped out. Why did he need a fantasy?

Wasn't she enough? Finally, he said he'd forget about her, but Emily never fully bought it. She'd seen her on campus and wondered. *What does this White woman have that I don't?* Maybe it all played into the fears her mother planted in her about mixed relationships, for she started to pick and nag at him, like her mother did to her. After Rory broke-up with her, she felt oddly relieved, even though she was broken hearted. She knew she had loved him, but maybe he never really loved her? She was left with doubts.

Falling in love with Sam was so unexpected to Emily that she had to think about whether it was really happening. It wasn't so much of an intellectual bond that they shared but fun. She laughed so much with him that he could have been a girlfriend to her like Jane. He was smart and intelligent. They could talk about anything and not fight about whose opinion was right. She found this refreshing after Rory, and he relied on her to be the philosophical one in the relationship, whereas he was the practical one. They had a nice symmetry together. Now, she was threatening to throw it all away.

It was almost noon and Emily was still at her desk, staring at the computer screen. *What am I going to do? Will he call?* Agitated, she went to the kitchen and jerked opened the cupboard and looked at the cans of soup, pasta, packages of instant noodles and slammed it closed. She tried the fridge next and shoved items around. *I hate it when Ma is right!* Images of Sam with a beautiful White woman filled her mind. Tears were streaming down her cheeks. *No!* She didn't want to believe her

184

mother's racist beliefs. *Sam loves me!* She shook her head, grabbed the phone and dialed before she could stop herself.

"Hello?" Sam picked up right away.

"Hi Sam, it's me," she tried calmly.

"Hi," he said flatly.

"Um...how was the movie last night?" Her heart pounded.

"It was okay."

"Good. I mean, I'm glad you stayed to watch it," she said with false cheer.

"Well, it wasn't much fun watching it alone," he said sarcastically.

"Oh...I'm sorry about that."

"What happened? Why did you just leave?"

"I guess that wasn't very nice of me, eh?" she said fidgeting.

"NO," he said quickly.

"Really, I am sorry Sam," she said earnestly. "I got upset and...it was stupid."

"YES, it was," he said. "We could have left together, don't you think?"

"Yes, you're right. I wasn't thinking, and I did want you to come over, I just...I don't know. It was dumb, really dumb." Her throat tightened and she struggled to get her words out. "Sorry. Really. I'm sorry."

Sam said nothing.

"Sam?" she said trying to keep her voice from shaking. "Are you...okay?"

"I don't know. I'm really pissed right now," he grumbled.

Emily brushed a tear away from her cheek.

"I mean I know you've been upset about your mother and her cancer, but you've been yelling at me and then that stupid thing last night...Do you want us to take a break or something?" he said.

Breakup? He wants to breakup? "No...No, Sam, please," she stuttered. "I don't know why I'm being such a jerk!"

"Well, maybe it would be better if we cancelled dinner with your mom and aunt tonight then, don't you think?"

Tears were raining down her face and she grabbed tissues to wipe her eyes. *He doesn't want to meet her?* She was consoled and hurt all at once. *What do I do?*

"I DO...do want you to...to meet my mother," she heard herself say surprising herself, "but I'm...I'm scared. Oh God, I'm so...so scared. It's stupid!" Emily gulped in some air. She saw Ma's angry face and heard her threats. *Would she really do it?* Emily didn't want to care and fought

186

angrily against the visions in her mind. *Let her kick me out and disown me!* Her strength against her mother's words suddenly gave out as she heard a child moaning, like she was in great pain. *Who was that?* This was all so ludicrous, but she couldn't stop. On the floor, she rocked and held herself in a fetal like position and continued this way until she heard the static from the phone and picked it back up.

"Oh Emily, don't cry, please," urged Sam. "Look, it's okay," he tried, "we'll have dinner tonight and...and, don't be scared."

Oh my God, that's me! She realized she had been making those awful sounds! Sam was still talking. *What did he say?* She held still.

"It's all okay, Emily," said Sam. "Do you still think dinner is a good idea tonight?"

He's still there. She sighed relieved. "Yes," she said tentatively at first, adding "I think it's time, Sam, like you suggested, to meet my mother," she was surprised by her own boldness.

"Are you going to be able to handle it?"

"Yes...I'm going to try," she said as she lifted her head up and stood tall. She recalled how Ma only came up to her chest.

"You're okay, really?" he asked.

"I think I am," she said still dumbfounded by her transformation.

"Okay, I'll pick you up at four o'clock," he said.

"I'll be ready."

The afternoon passed quickly. Emily finished her laundry and tried to write reports. *How were things going to go?* she kept wondering, disrupting her concentration on work. Although she had lots of experience hiding things from her mother or fighting with her, she never put much thought into when she would stop hiding or fighting with her. In fact, she never even dreamed of this day really happening, when her mother would sit down happily with her boyfriend? *Not after Rory.* Well, maybe she occasionally slipped and fantasized about having a tête-à-tête moment, like on *The Brady Bunch*, but after she was married. *Fat chance!* All she could imagine was Ma's long face throughout dinner. She chased the image away, reminding herself that Auntie Sue and Sam were there. Ma could be silent all night and the three of them could enjoy themselves! Satisfied by this image, she turned off her computer. It was 3:30 and Sam would be coming soon.

She had already decided on a pair of tan pants and a black sweater to wear for dinner. In the bathroom she picked up her toothbrush and freshened up. Then she studied her face to see if she needed any touching up. She reapplied the eye makeup that she had cried it off earlier, dabbed some more blush onto her cheeks and powdered her face. Just as she finished, she heard a knock on the door, followed by the sound of the door being unlocked.

"Sam?" she called out.

"Hi," he said appearing at her bedroom doorway. Sam was wearing a red V-neck sweater and black cotton pants.

"You look nice," she said approvingly and moved into his arms for a kiss. She lingered in his soft mouth and held him tightly. They smiled at each other as their lips released.

"Hmm, you like nice too," he said with a grin. "Are you okay?"

"I think I am," she said trying to sound confident.

"Okay, let's go."

She grabbed her jean jacket and purse and locked the door behind them. They walked out of the building, arms hooked together to his car. As they drove towards the restaurant, she talked nervously about what happened to her as she did laundry in the morning. "I would never do that; take someone's wet laundry out of the machine, would you? Next time, maybe I should bring a book and read while I wait for my laundry to be done, eh?"

"Guess you could," he said with a smile and added, "that kind of stuff happens all the time, don't you think?"

"Guess so," she said seeing the familiar sign of the Best Wokk Restaurant in front of her. "It's just not nice, that's all."

He nodded as he turned into the parking lot and parked the car.

She looked at the three cars that were already parked, but did not see Auntie Sue's red Pontiac there. "They're not here yet," she said trying to relax, as she checked for cars at the entranceway.

"Should we go get a table?" Sam asked.

"Sure," she said jumping out of the car. They went into the empty restaurant and sat at a table for four, facing the westerly driveway. Clear glass windows surrounded the restaurant from the back where the parking lot was and lined the driveway to the east of the restaurant. "Have a look at the menus," she said handing him a large regular menu and a small one labelled Chef Specials.

"Lots of choices," Sam said flipping the pages. "What's good here?"

"My mom likes to have fish, chicken and vegetables. I like having the sweet and sour pork and this dish," she said pointing at a breaded grouper fish with cream corn sauce. Her heart was beating like she had had too much coffee and she couldn't stop staring out the window. *Where is she?* She kept her eyes on the driveway, glancing down every now and then at the menu to point out familiar dishes. A red car stopped by the entranceway, and she saw her mother descend from the car. "She's here, she's here," she said springing up from her seat and walking briskly towards the front door. "Ma," she called out, pushing the door open. Her mother walked in, and Emily took her by the arm and led her towards Sam, who had stood up at their table. She looked at Sam's smiling face and composed herself.

"Ma, this is Sam," she said as they came up to the table.

"Jeu siem, nice to meet you," he said grabbing her mother's hand and shaking it.

"Hello," said Ma with a wry grin at Sam, as they both helped her take a seat.

She ignored her mother's face and saw Auntie Sue beaming as she came to their table.

"This is my Aunt Sue," Emily said as Sam stood up to shake her hand.

"Nice to meet you, Aunt Sue," he said smiling.

"Oh, so nice to meet you Sam," she said still grinning and standing. "I heard you speak Chinese? You speak well! You hear him speak Big Sister?" she asked Ma.

Ma nodded and seemed to smirk. Emily was dumbfounded. *Is she smiling?*

"Oh, Emily, he is so good looking!" Auntie Sue said, causing Emily to blush.

"Thank you," Sam said laughing.

Auntie Sue giggled, let go of Sam's hand and they both sat down. "So what do you want to eat?" she asked as she opened a menu.

"Please, why don't you and Mrs. Chow order for us?" he said as he looked at Ma and Auntie Sue. "I eat everything."

"Really?" Auntie Sue said as she giggled and whispered something to Ma. "I see live shrimp in the fish tank. Do you like shrimp, Sam?"

"Oh yes."

Ma nodded as she and Auntie Sue discussed what to order. Auntie Sue waved a waitress over. After she ordered the last dish, she asked Emily, "Is there anything else you would like?"

"Just sweet and sour pork," she said.

Auntie Sue added that to the order, before she picked up the cup of hot tea that Sam had poured for her. She took a sip and smiled. Emily smiled back and looked at her mother who was staring silently down at the white plastic tablecloth. *Just what I expected.* She looked away, but felt a gentle squeeze at the knee from underneath the table. Sam's tender look softened her.

"So Ma," she tried, "what did you and Auntie Sue do yesterday?"

Ma looked at her and shrugged. "Just stay home. Not much to do." Her lip was pulled into a pout.

That pout! Emily tried to overlook it and glanced at her aunt for help.

"You forgot we went for a walk!" Auntie Sue jumped in on cue. "It was a beautiful day, wasn't it?" Everyone at the table nodded.

"So, Emily tells me you like to garden?" Sam tried to talk to Ma.

Ma nodded.

"Ah, what are you growing this year?"

"Nothing," said Ma. "Too tired."

"But I helped you," said Auntie Sue nudging Ma. "I planted some spinach, snow peas and bok choy."

"Mmm," Sam said nodding.

"Um, Sam's dad likes to garden too," Emily added.

"Really? What does your dad like to grow?" Auntie Sue asked excitedly.

"Oh, he loves to garden. He planted sweet peas, tomatoes and lettuce this year."

"Good, good," Auntie Sue said nodding and nudging Ma again, who was still staring at the tablecloth.

Ma looked up as if woken by Auntie Sue's prompting. She scrutinized Sam and asked, "So, you have good job, Sam?"

"Yes ma'am, I work for Price Waterhouse, a very good company."

"You make lots of money, Sam?" she asked.

"Ma! You can't ask that!" Emily said hotly. *How dare she?*

Sam laughed. "It's okay," he said to Emily, and with a serious voice, he said to Ma, "I make very good money."

Emily was taken by surprise. Sam was playing her!

"Enough to take care of my daughter?" Ma asked.

"Ma!" she protested.

"Yes," he said nodding. "Enough to take care of Emily." He reached over to touch her hand, but she withdrew it.

Ma nodded satisfied and stopped the interrogation. The waitress came up to their table with their first dish: cooked shrimp with dipping sauce.

"Here Sam," Auntie Sue said after she had served some shrimp to Ma, "take some."

Sam picked up a shrimp with his chopsticks.

"You use chopsticks! Good!" Auntie Sue said clapping. "Now you eat it like this," Auntie Sue said as she peeled the shell, dipped the shrimp in the sauce and popped it into her mouth.

"Okay," he said as he started to peel his shrimp.

"And the head, don't waste the head!" she added as she took it and sucked out the contents.

Emily looked at Sam who was chewing his first shrimp. "Don't be silly, Auntie Sue," she scolded and took the shrimp head off of Sam's plate.

"No, no," he said. "I want to try." He took it back.

Everyone stared as Sam brought the pointy, orange head with its long whiskers and tiny white eyes, to his lips and sipped.

"Not bad," he finally said. "But I think I've had enough." He put the shrimp head down.

Emily tried to hide her smile behind a napkin, but Auntie Sue laughed out loud and poked Ma, who had been watching. She had a grin. Sam had managed to make her mother smile! Her fear dissipated and she felt something she didn't think she'd ever feel. *Was it acceptance?* She wasn't really sure, but it was nice.

When the remaining dishes had been doggie bagged for Auntie Sue and Ma, Emily gave the waitress the familiar signature sign and waited for her to bring the bill. The waitress came back with four bowls of red bean soup and placed the black plastic bill tray between Emily and Sam.

"Give me the bill," Auntie Sue said as she reached over.

"No, no," Emily said, as she put her credit card down. "It's our treat."

"Yes," said Sam agreeing as he replaced Emily's credit card with his and handed the bill tray to a server. "It's our treat."

"Sam..." she protested.

"Please," he said. "I'm happy to take everyone out for dinner," and he grinned at Auntie Sue and Ma.

"Sam, it was very nice to meet you!" Auntie Sue said with a broad smile. "Thank you for the dinner!"

"You're welcome," he said as he looked down to sign the returned Visa bill.

Emily looked at her mother who was moving out of her chair. Ma stood up, picked up her new black purse and looked straight at her. *She wasn't pouting.* Emily had to stop her mouth from gaping. She watched Ma slowly walk around the table and stop in front of Sam. A sudden surge of nausea overcame her.

"Sam," she said and she held out her hand. "Thank you for dinner and taking care of my daughter."

"It's my pleasure, Mrs. Chow," Sam said as he stood up and shook Ma's hand. "You have a beautiful daughter, and I plan to always take care of her."

What did he say? Emily was having a hard time hearing with the loud thudding in her chest.

"He is so nice," Auntie Sue whispered as she put her arms around her and squeezed. Emily felt her breath release, and she took another one in, as she began to relax.

"Yes, he is," she said and she hugged Auntie Sue's right arm.

Ma had already started walking. "Let's go." she said. Auntie Sue nodded and walked quickly to catch up to Ma. Sam came around to Emily, took her hand and they slowly walked towards the door.

"Thank you," said the waitress with a smile. They both smiled back and pushed the doors open to the waiting crowds. It was 6:30 now and every table in the restaurant was full. They jostled their way through families and couples until they were outside. Emily could see Ma and Auntie Sue getting into their car. She pulled at Sam's arm, but by the time they reached the car, her mother was already seated

"Ma!" she called. Ma rolled down the window.

"It was nice to meet you, Jeu siem," Sam said as he grabbed Ma's hand and shook it again.

Ma nodded and waved goodbye as Auntie Sue turned the car on.

"Bye, Sam," Auntie Sue called out with a big smile.

They stood back and watched, arm in arm, as Ma and Auntie Sue drove away. Emily observed the scene: cars fighting for parking spaces, people getting in and out of their cars. Most of the people were Asian. She felt their eyes on them, but she didn't care. She kept on smiling.

Chapter Fifteen

On Monday evening, as she settled down for dinner she picked up the phone. Emily had been thinking about last night's dinner all day. *Did Ma really approve of Sam? Maybe she was pretending?* She didn't know. Sam was sure. He thought the dinner was a huge success. She wanted to believe this too and so she dialed home.

"Hello?"

"Ma?"

"Emily?"

"Yeah, it's me. Have you had dinner yet?" Emily felt that lump in her throat return.

"Yes, we had the rest of the food from dinner yesterday and some fresh vegetables," Ma said calmly.

"Hmm..." she said. "And did you like dinner?"

"Oh yes, the food very good yesterday."

"Uh huh," she said and waited for her mother to say more.

"Well," Ma finally said. "I come to Toronto tomorrow see Dr. Lee."

"Oh," she said disappointed and paused. "What other days are you coming into town?"

"Tuesday, Thursday and Friday."

"Okay...well maybe I'll come by the clinic on one of those days," Emily said to make conversation.

"Really? Which one?"

"I'm not sure yet, Ma!" she said testily.

"Okay, okay," her mother responded. "Do you want to speak with Auntie Sue?"

"Sure," she said resigned. "Put her on." She waited while Ma called for her aunt. *Did she like Sam or not?* It seemed doubtful.

"Hello?"

"Hi Auntie Sue," she said dully.

"Oh, Emily, Sam is so nice and so handsome," she gushed.

She smiled and flushed. "Thank you, Auntie Sue," she said relieved.

"Your Ma is so happy for you!" she continued.

"Really? She didn't say anything to me," she said despondently. "In fact, I'm not so sure she likes him at all!"

"You know how your Ma is right? She said to me that Sam is tall."

"Uh huh."

"And that he has a good job."

"Uh huh. Anything else?"

"Yes, that he probably makes good money."

"Okay..."

"So she is very happy for you!"

"She said that?"

"What? Oh, Emily you know how your Ma is, but I know she is very happy for you. I can see it in her eyes."

She sighed. "Well thanks, Auntie Sue. I have to go now."

"Okay. Will see you this week?"

"Yes, I will try to drop by the clinic. What time are the appointments?"

"Ten o'clock in the morning."

"Okay, I'll see you then," she said and hung up. She looked at her cold dinner, took a bite of the pasta and put her fork down. *He's tall, has a good job and makes good money. So?* Emily still didn't know what to think. She got up, found the plastic wrap and nuked her food. Comforted, she ate.

As she was eating, she recalled how she tried to get close to her mother when she was young. Maybe she was 12 or 13 years old? So many television shows depicted this intimate mother-daughter relationship that she had no idea about, like *The Brady Bunch* or *Eight is Enough*. Her mother wasn't the touchy feely type. No hugs or "I love you" growing up. In fact, Emily didn't even know how to say these three words in Chinese even if she wanted to! She wasn't sure if any of her friends had this type of idyllic sitcom relationship, but the programs made her feel defective, like something wasn't right in her family. If she could only find the right moment or words, something magical would happen between her mother and herself. She was convinced of it or at least she was led to believe this. When she started to menstruate, she was sure her mom would give her "the talk" and they would hug and cry. Nope. Ma just took out a box of pads, told her to soak and wash her underwear and to make sure her father didn't see any of this woman stuff. A year later, she tried again and asked her mom about tampons and how to use them because she was going swimming. Her mom just looked at the tampon in disgust and told her "don't use" them. Disappointed yet again, she stopped trying. *Maybe it fed her teenaged anger?* Silly. All these years later, she still fantasized about something that doesn't exit. She chided herself, got up and took her dishes to the kitchen.

The next day after she finished her morning routine, she dutifully got into her car and drove to Dr. Lee's neighbourhood. Yesterday, as she worked, she continued to have daydreams of either her mother yelling and screaming, or smiling lovingly at her. It was exhausting, these fantasies, but she didn't know how to let go of them. *How do you let it go?* She wasn't even sure she wanted to see her mother today and yet found herself organizing her schedule around her mother's appointment. *What's going to happen?* Likely nothing. It was 10:30 when she parked and walked towards the clinic. Ma should be full of needles by now, she thought to herself as she pulled open the weighted door.

"Your mother is in room two," Auntie Sue whispered from the sunken couch.

She nodded and proceeded in. She knocked on the door labelled #2 before opening it. "Ma?" she called.

"Emily?" responded Ma.

The light had been dimmed, but she could see her mother resting on the bed with needles pulsating throughout her body. Ma was frowning. *Oh God. Here it comes.* It didn't look good and she resisted the familiar urge to strike first. She took a seat by the head of the bed and waited.

"Emily, Emily-a."

"Yes, Ma?" she said trying to stay calm.

"You really like that goi-law?"

"Yes, Ma." Sarcasm slipped out before she could stop herself and she added, "Sam, his name is Sam!"

Ma shook her head. "Ai...what can do? My English not so good. How to talk to his parents?"

Is Ma trying? She wanted to be empathetic, but all she could think of is why didn't you learn more English? "Does that really matter Ma?" she asked.

Her mother sighed. "You don't understand. You born here."

"Yes, yes I was born here," she said. "So what?" Her mother was doing it again. Highlighting their cultural differences and making her feel guilty even though she didn't know why she should. Why did it always come down to this? Are kids born in China really so good and kids born here so bad?

"Okay, okay," Ma, said motioning her to quiet down.

She sat back down and stared at the flickering red light of the electrical stimulation machine, feeling drained. *I don't want to fight anymore.* She studied the brass door handle and imagined running for it, but she couldn't move. Not this time. Something made her stay. After what felt like an eternity, Ma spoke again.

"He is nice man. Good person."

She looked at her mother stunned.

"I wish he Chinese."

She felt her blood rushing again, but kept quiet.

"But your life. Your choice. What I can do?"

She stared at her mother to see what would come next. Instead, Ma closed her eyes. Her mouth was drawn to a close. The conversation was finished. *This was her acceptance?* Dr. Lee interrupted Emily's ambivalent thoughts, by entering the room with a smile.

"Hello Emily," he said grinning as he turned the machine off, detached the connections and started to remove needles.

"Hi, Dr. Lee," she said, "Are you going to give her some Chi next?"

"Yes," he said with a wink as he quickly finished up the moxibustion.

"Ma, I'm leaving now okay?"

Her mother opened her eyes, looked at her and nodded, before closing them again.

She picked up her purse and left the room.

"Goodbye, Auntie Sue," she said softly to her aunt, who was resting her head against her bent wrist.

"Oh," Auntie Sue said with a start, "you going now?"

She nodded and waved as she pushed the door open and walked out.

Chapter Sixteen

Emily had an extremely busy week. She saw a client daily and wrote a report every night. On Friday after her last assessment of the week, she worked on a report until four o'clock, then turned her computer off and moved herself to the living room to watch a bit of Oprah before getting herself ready for dinner at Jane's. Jane had been dating this guy named Steve recently and wanted Emily's opinion of him. She walked to the bathroom to freshen up during commercials. During the first one, she brushed her teeth. In the subsequent ones, she freshened up her face and put some more hairspray in her hair. It was almost five o'clock and Oprah was wrapping up when she heard keys unlocking the front door.

"In here Sam," she called from the couch.

"Hey," he said coming around the corner with a Dufflet Pastries cake box in his hand.

"What did you pick up?"

"Something chocolate, like you said."

"Good and thanks," she said.

"Tired?" he asked as he bent down to give her a kiss.

"Oh yeah," she said. "You?"

"Sure," he said as he sat down beside her and picked up the remote control. "Can I flip?"

"Sure," she said. "My show is done anyways. Want something to drink?"

"Okay."

Emily pulled herself up and walked to the kitchen. She took out a can of iced tea from the fridge, snapped it open and poured it into two glasses. She walked back to the living room where Sam had settled on a business channel.

"Here," she said handing him a glass.

"Thanks," he said taking a sip. "So, what time are we supposed to be there?"

"Six o'clock," she said as she looked down at her wristwatch.

"Hmm..." he said, eyes focused straight ahead.

"So..." she said. "Should we go in ten?"

He nodded his head.

She sipped her drink and watched as the symbols and numbers floated by. After her conversation with her mother on Monday, she didn't bother to visit her during her subsequent appointments at Dr. Lee's clinic. Of course, she called her every night or every other night. Ma talked about what she did or ate. Sam never came up. Auntie Sue assured her that everything was well. *Let it be.* She went back to the status quo. What did she expect, really? They had their talk about Sam, but nothing really miraculous happened between herself and her mother, right? Jane told her that her reaction was strange. On the phone Tuesday evening, she had given Jane the play by play of Sunday's dinner and of her visit to the clinic Monday.

"You did it!" Jane said proudly. "You've been so scared and worried and look what happened!"

"Yes," said Emily slowly. "I guess I had no choice but to tell her, right?"

"No, you did more than that!" exclaimed Jane. "You faced one of your fears!"

Emily tried to digest what her friend had said. She was right, but why was she so unsatisfied? Jane continued with her accolades, eventually boosting Emily's morale. She recognized she did do something important, and yet something still seemed to be missing. Ma would never become her best friend like Jane was with her mother. She knew this. After all these years of the same mother-daughter dance, she and Ma had taken a new step. *Shouldn't she feel good?* "Damned, crazy *Brady Bunch*!" she thought. It was only a television series and not reality. *Stupid.* Although something had happened between herself and her mother. She felt cheated. *Weren't they acting the same?*

Glancing at her watch, she elbowed Sam and said, "Let's go."

"Okay," Sam said as he turned the television off.

They left the apartment, descended the outside stairs and walked towards Sam's car. Yellow tulips lined the front of the apartment building, their petals fully extended to drink in the warmth of the sun. The grass looked thick and green, requiring weekly cuts. Emily took her navy blazer off and held Sam's hand until she had to go round to the passenger side. She let herself in after the door had been unlocked and belted herself up.

"Front and Jarvis, here we go again!" Sam joked.

Jane loved to entertain and she was a great cook. They tried to take turns hosting dinners for events like Thanksgiving. Emily enjoyed it too, but got a bit stressed with the planning and preparation. Back in university, when they were living together off campus, they bought cookbooks and practiced making new recipes. Jane seemed to have a natural flare for it, whereas, Emily struggled and fumbled with it. After that rice fiasco in first year, she honed her skills in easy Chinese cooking since she was a disaster in baking. One time she left the salt out of banana loaf, thinking it didn't need it. Wrong. It didn't rise the way it

210

was supposed to and was bland and hard. She attempted to make cookies – too tough; muffins – too flat. Finally, she gave up and stuck to cooking. Jane goofed up too and some fancy dishes that took hours of preparation went straight to the trash. For New Year's Day dinner, Jane made prawn bisque from a Julia Childs' cookbook. Her sister called it "interesting" and her coworker said it was "rich" before it was cleared from the table for the main course.

"So how was your day?" Emily asked Sam as he drove.

"Pretty good," he said as he recounted the funny stories of the day, making her chuckle.

Traffic was light and he maneuvered easily downtown to Jane's condominium. They paid for parking underneath the building and walked up the concrete stairs towards the front of the building. The concierge let them in as he recognized Emily, and they took the elevator up to the twelfth floor. She knocked at Jane's front door and waited.

"Hi!" Jane said opening the door. Her black and white cat stood there to greet them in as well. Emily hugged and kissed her friend, as did Sam, before removing their shoes. Steve was tall and slim; his blond brushed cut hair framed his potato-shaped head.

"This is Steve," Jane said in introduction as they both took turns shaking Steve's hand.

"Why don't you guys take a seat? Can I get you a drink?" Jane offered.

Sam agreed to some wine, while Emily opted for a glass of juice. They followed her past the dark wooden dining room table, to the rust-coloured couch. Jane had put out a tray of cut pita bread with baba ganouche and some cheese and crackers on the ottoman. Steve and Jane took a seat on the couch, so she and Sam sat opposite each other in the large armchairs that encircled the couch.

"So...how has your week been going, Emily?" Jane asked.

She nodded her head since she had just stuffed a piece of cheese into it. She waited until her mouth was almost empty before answering. "Okay. It's been busy with seeing clients, reports, you know, the usual stuff. How about yours?" As Jane spoke, she noticed that Sam and Steve, who were adjacent to each other, were starting to talk. She waited until her friend finished speaking, before turning her attention to them.

"Yeah, that's a good team." Sam nodded in agreement and reached for more pita and dip.

"So what do you do, Steve?" Emily asked eager to engage him.

"I'm a student actually, just finishing up teacher's college." Steve replied, turning his attention to her.

"Great," she said. "What grades are you planning to teach?"

"The younger school grades like 1 and 2."

"Wow, little kids, eh?" Sam said.

"Yeah, I like the little ones."

"I would find that tough," Sam said.

"Actually, they're great," Steve said. "They're very impressionable, and I like being able to shape young minds."

"Is that how you two met? In school?" Emily knew the whole story already, but wanted to keep the conversation rolling.

"Yes," they said both nodding and smiling.

"Well it was in the library..." Jane said with a laugh.

"And?" she asked, tauntingly.

"I was doing some research for my paper..."

"She's always in the library," Emily quipped.

"And I saw this cute guy studying..."

"I'm in the library a lot too!" Steve added.

"So I sat down at the table next to him and..."

"She offered me a piece of gum."

"Nice pick up line, Jane," Sam teased.

"I was wondering like did I stink or something, you know?" Steve said laughing.

Jane started to howl, as did Emily at this. "Luckily, he was not insulted by my gum offer, and we started to chat," Jane continued, once she stopped laughing.

"Other people at the table started to give us dirty looks," Steve said. "So I suggested we go for coffee and well...here we are." He pulled Jane closer to him, as his arm had been wrapped around her waist, and gave her a small kiss.

Emily smiled content. It was nice to see her friend so happy.

They finished the bread and most of the dip before Jane called everyone to the dining room table. Steve was vegetarian, but ate seafood. Jane had placed a large oval platter with pasta in tomato sauce, surrounded by steamed mussels on the table.

"Mmm...that looks delicious Jane!" Emily said seeing her friend chose to make something she'd perfected. Everyone agreed and they all sat down.

"Here, let me pour you some wine," Steve said pouring the Shiraz they had brought.

"Cheers," said Jane as they raised their wine glasses and voices in unison.

After dinner, they took the mocha cake or "cakelet" as it was called, to the living room to enjoy. Jane served tea.

"That was an excellent dinner, Jane." Sam said.

"Yeah, she's a great cook," complimented Steve. "Thank you, Sweetie," he said as he bent down to kiss her.

"Mmm...you're welcome," Jane purred before locking lips with him.

Emily grinned and smiled at Sam. He was perfect for Jane, just like Sam was for her. "Okay, who wants cake?" she asked.

"Please," said Steve after he released Jane.

"Me too," added Jane.

Emily cut into the moist brown cake and placed one-inch pieces onto four plates. "Don't be shy," she said as she helped herself to a plate and moved back to her seat. "This is Sam's favourite cake."

"Well, for the moment," responded Sam.

"It's very good," said Jane after her first bite. Steve nodded in agreement.

"What do you mean by your favourite cake for the moment?" Jane asked. "For as long as I've known you, you've always wanted mocha cake."

"Well, you never know when another cake might come along to replace it," Sam said smiling.

"You trying to leave yourself open to options?" Jane teased.

"With cake, yes. With women, no," Sam said blowing a kiss at Emily. "Because once you've got the perfect fit, what else do you need?" he asked.

Emily felt instantly hot, but was pleased. "Oh please," she cried, "you're such a ham!"

"Oh come on, Em," said Jane, "I think he's being sweet."

"Yes," she said feeling enamored, "yes, he is." Sam's face was lit up, and she grinned back at him. Sam never had any problems showing his affection to her in public or in private.

They sipped their tea and ate their cake. It was almost midnight before Emily and Sam left. She hadn't thought of her mother until that time, but knew it was too late to call. Besides, she had spoken to her the previous night. Outside, Sam carried her piggyback style to the car, since she said she was too tired to walk. His playfulness prolonged her joyful mood. Back at her apartment, their lovemaking seemed even more intense than after dinner with Ma. Emily lay back, letting Sam take command of her body. She moaned out loudly, unconcerned about the neighbours. Afterwards, she fell into a dreamless sleep.

Chapter Seventeen

The phone rang repeatedly and then the answering machine went on. Emily opened her eyes and could see signs of daylight coming through the window. She reached for the clock she kept at her night table: 5 am.

"Emily, I'm sorry to wake you. Please WAKE UP! It's your auntie," called the excited voice through the answering machine.

It was Auntie Sue. She bounded out of bed, instantly awake and ran to the kitchen where the answering machine was. She stopped and grabbed the phone receiver. "Hello?" she said breathless, "Auntie Sue?"

"Yes, it's me. I'm sorry to wake you, but it's, it's your Ma..."

"What is it? What's wrong?" she said as her heart raced.

"We're at the hospital. Something happened last night. We were in the living room after supper and she got up to go the bathroom...and then she just fell to the ground. I called 911. I tried to give her oxygen, you know like what I saw on television and breathed into her mouth. The ambulance guy said that I saved her." Auntie Sue sounded frantic.

"When? What time did this happen?" she asked confused.

"Around eleven o'clock last night."

"You've been at the hospital all night? Why didn't you call me earlier?"

"Your uncle came to the hospital too, and we decided not to disturb you until morning." Auntie Sue explained.

"Okay, we're coming. You're at Trafalgar General Hospital right? See you soon," she said and hung up. *What's happening?* She wondered if she was having a bad dream.

Sam had gotten out of bed and was standing in the doorway staring at her. She felt the tears welling. "My mom's in the hospital. We have to go now."

He nodded and asked, "Did she have a heart attack?"

"I'm not sure. It sounds like she collapsed." She walked straight into the bathroom and turned on the water. Her head ached from last night's wine and she needed a quick rinse to freshen up, before they rushed out to Sam's car.

Even with the cold shower, Emily didn't feel like she was awake. She didn't know what to think. *Wasn't Ma getting better? Is this a dream?*

She was certain that this was minor and that everything would be fine. It *had* to be. "Sam, let's grab some coffee and muffins." she said trying to keep this event casual.

"Okay," he said and went through the drive-thru to get the food faster.

Fear was flourishing despite her earlier conviction that everything was fine. Questions flew through her mind like "What happened?" and "Did I miss something when I saw Ma last?" She was afraid to verbalize her fears. *What if saying them makes them real?* Instead, she tried to appear stoic, as she held onto Sam's hand. She didn't realize how hard she was squeezing his hand, until he broke free of her grip.

"Easy, easy," he said patting her hand. "It'll be all right," he said as he returned his free hand to her possession. She hung on, thankful for his support.

Very few cars were on the highway this bright and sunny day. Sam drove quickly and within twenty minutes they were decelerating off the highway. She directed him until they reached the hospital parking lot and parked the car.

At Emergency, they walked down a long beige corridor and through double steel doors labelled Restricted. The nurse led them to Auntie Sue and a bedridden Ma.

"Auntie Sue," Emily said as she approached. Her aunt looked up after she finished wiping her mother's face with a damp cloth. Ma's eyes were closed, but a yellow tube was around her mouth, connected to a machine that made a pumping sound. Ma's chest rose and fell as oxygen was pumped into her tiny body. She looked pale, and her right arm was purple and bruised where the intravenous was. Above her head, a monitor beeped and displayed the beating of her heart. *What's going on? Is she okay?* A lump seemed stuck in Emily's throat, preventing her from speaking. She trembled. Sam held her tight.

"Ai Emily," said Auntie Sue sadly.

"You look tired," she said turning her attention to her aunt.

A nurse walked in and removed a near empty sack from the IV pole. She hooked up a new clear bag and smiled at them and said, "Your aunt is taking such good care of your mother."

"Thank you," Auntie Sue replied.

"Dr. Goldberg is coming to speak with you," she said before leaving the room.

Emily stared at her mother. *When is she going to wake up?* She looked at the compressor sending air into her mother's body, then up at the monitor. Auntie Sue continued to gingerly wipe Ma's face. Sam stood close by. *Is this a dream?* It appeared to be a scene from a soap opera, not something happening in real life, in *her* life. Pressure mounted in her head. *What is going on, what is going on...*

A short stocky man in a white lab coat walked towards them. He wore glasses, had wavy brown hair, mustache and a beard. He extended his hand out as he introduced himself as Dr. Goldberg.

"Let's go into the Family Meeting Room," he said, "I'd like to discuss your mother's situation with you." They left Ma behind and followed him out of the double doors and into a room with a long black oval shaped table and chairs. The doctor closed the door, sat at the head of the table and opened a brown file.

"Your mother is not doing well," he began.

"What do you mean?" Emily asked feeling agitated.

"She was diagnosed with liver cancer, right?" he asked.

"Yes."

"Well, it appears the cancer metastasized and spread...almost exploded throughout her body. Her body just couldn't take it anymore, so she collapsed."

Emily shook her head. She stared at Dr. Goldberg's face in disbelief. *This can't be happening! I've got to talk with Dr. Lee.* She clutched at her elbows and started to rock.

"What can we do?" she finally managed to say after she was calmer.

"Well, we have two choices. First choice is that we wait to see if her condition will improve. We will keep her on life support, but there is nothing else we can really do for her."

She nodded and waited.

"The second option and the one that I recommend, is that we disconnect her from life support and..."

"What? We can't do that yet, we have to wait!" Emily yelled cutting him off.

"Yes, please," Auntie Sue pleaded. "Let's give her some more time to see if she'll recover."

"I have no problem with that," Dr. Goldberg said. "But please keep an open mind as we'll revisit our decision later." He stood up and closed the file.

Auntie Sue got up, shook Dr. Goldberg's hand and thanked him for his help. Emily didn't bother, and she practically bowled him down as she strut back through the double doors to her mother's bedside. *How dare he! Ma's going to get better!* Sam caught up with her, and together they kept watch of her mother. Click, the compressor sounded as oxygen was pumped into her mother's frail body. *Dr. Lee, Dr. Lee. I have to speak to you!* She felt Sam's hand squeeze her left shoulder, and she leaned into his warm body.

"Why don't you go home for a few hours?" the nurse suggested from behind them.

"Is that all right?" Auntie Sue asked.

"Of course. We will take care of her."

Emily looked at her aunt. Her eyes were red and swollen, her shoulders were slouched, and she looked disheveled. "Yes, let's take Auntie Sue home to get some rest," she said to Sam who nodded.

"What time should we return?" she asked the nurse.

"Anytime," she said.

"Okay, can you let Dr. Goldberg know we will be back later?"

"Of course."

She turned around, touched her mother's hand lightly and said to her, "we'll be back soon." Auntie Sue also spoke to Ma before the three of them walked away. Dichotomous feelings of relief and anxiety arose as they left the Restricted area. *Will Ma be okay?* Still, she couldn't wait to get away.

"Code Blue, Code Blue," was being called over the PA system as they left the hospital and walked towards their cars.

In the parking lot, Emily offered to take her aunt to her own home to get some rest. After some initial protesting, she agreed, but insisted on driving there herself.

"I'll come over at lunch time to fix you something to eat," Auntie Sue said from her car.

"Don't be silly," Emily said. "Just come over after you get some rest, okay?"

Auntie Sue nodded and drove off. They walked over to Sam's car and she let herself into the passenger side. Her body felt heavy, drained as she leaned back against the headrest. She watched herself lift her arm, as if she was doing this in slow motion and looked at her watch: 9:30. They drove in silence until they reached her home. Fumbling through her purse for house keys, she stumbled upon Dr. Lee's business card and woke up. Inside, she kicked her shoes off, looked for the cordless phone and dialed the number on the card. She sat at the kitchen table, drumming her free fingers and waited as the phone rang once, twice, seven times before the answering machine finally kicked in.

"Dr. Lee, it's me Emily. Can you please call me? My mother is in the hospital. The phone number here is 905-848-2278. A...thanks," she said as she hung up.

"Trying to reach Dr. Lee?" Sam asked.

She nodded. "Yes, I'd like some advice from him." Bothered, she got up and walked to the fridge. She looked in and grabbed some juice. "Want some?" she asked.

"Sure."

She poured two glasses of orange juice and brought them over to the table. She sipped the cold juice, put her glass down, walked back to the fridge and looked in again. *Where is he?* Sam had picked up the newspaper and was looking through the front section. She slammed the fridge closed, walked into the living room and turned on the television. She flipped through the channels, turned the television off and on, then walked back into the kitchen and sat down opposite Sam. He looked up at her.

"I have to get a hold of Dr. Lee," she finally said.

"I know," he said quietly.

She stood up and added, "She was doing well in treatment, she was getting stronger...he'll know what to do!" She looked at her watch: 10:00. The clinic is now open. He'll call, she thought to herself recalling how busy the clinic was when it opened on a Saturday.

She walked back into the living room and stood in the doorway. Straight ahead of her was the television with Saturday morning cartoons playing. To her left against the wall that separated the living room from the kitchen was a black leather couch, with the matching loveseat on the opposite wall. The club chair was to her right against the wall with the window. Ma liked to sit on the couch with one of her crocheted blankets on her lap. She kept her hands warm by tucking them under the blanket as she watched television. Her dad liked to sit in the club chair with one leg up on his seat as he watched. The washroom was outside the doorway at end of the couch. Emily traced Ma's path from her usual seat on the couch towards the washroom. She studied the thin gray carpet for clues for where Ma collapsed. None could be found. Next, she lay down on the ground at the end of the couch in front of the doorway by the bathroom. *Was this where Ma was?* The floor felt hard despite the carpet. She extended her arms out along the ground, turned her palms up as she had done in yoga, in corpse position and closed her eyes. She imagined her mother lying in this exact location with Auntie Sue and the paramedics around her. *Oh my God! Ma!* Hot tears spilled from her eyes, and she started to shake. She jumped up quickly, muffled her mouth and ran into the washroom.

With the door closed, she turned the facet on as well as the bathroom fan to block the howling sounds coming from within her. *This can't be happening!* She sat on the toilet to pee, struggling to regulate her breath. Someone knocked at the door.

"Emily? Are you okay?" Sam asked.

"Yes," she said with a steady voice. She blew her nose one more time before she opened the door. "I'm fine," she said to him, but Sam pulled her into his arms. She felt strengthened by his touch.

"I was thinking that Ma was here," she said pointing to the ground. He shuddered, and they slowly moved towards the formal living room at the front of the house. They sat down on the stiff floral couch. A large floor to ceiling window allowed plenty of sunlight into this room, and Ma had placed most of her sun loving plants here. She leaned her head into Sam's neck and closed her eyes. Sam embraced her tightly, and she felt her body jerk, as she opened her eyes.

"I fell to sleep?" she asked.

"Yep," he said laughing.

"Mmm...that neck of yours is so comfortable," she said snuggling again into it for a few seconds. She looked at her watch. It was almost eleven o'clock now. She got up. *No phone call yet.* Her stomach churned.

"Are you hungry?" he asked. "We can go get some lunch."

"Yeah, maybe that would be a good idea, but what if Auntie Sue comes over?"

"Why don't you just call and leave her a message?"

"But I don't want to wake her if she's sleeping."

"Okay," said Sam. "I'll just go out and pick up some food for everybody."

"Sure." She agreed and watched Sam put his shoes on.

"Subs or something like that okay?" he asked as he opened the front door.

"Sounds good," she said anxiously locking the door after him. She looked at her watch again, then marched into the living room and picked up the phone. Seated in the club chair, she waited while the phone rang, once, twice, followed by the answering machine. She fiddled with her hair as she waited for Dr. Lee's message to finish.

"Dr. Lee," she said, "it's me, Emily. I left you a message earlier. Can you please call me? My mother is in the hospital. My phone number again is 905-848-2278. Ah...thanks," she said hanging up the phone. *Dr. Lee!* Sighing out loud, she pushed herself up and wandered, arms crossed over her chest. She found herself cautiously walking up the spiral stairs until she reached the top landing. To her left was her bedroom, beside the rosy pink bathroom, and the guest room where Auntie Sue was staying came next. Her parent's bedroom was on the right, and she entered the opened door. Ma's mirrored bureau stood to the left of her, and she found herself staring at the reflection in the mirror. *I look like shit.*

She looked at her mother's bed. The golden bedspread was still neatly tucked under the double pillows. On the headboard shelf, Big Ben, with its large brown face, was still ticking away. It was 11:30. She looked back at the dresser and pulled open the right side drawer. To her surprise, the old jewelry box she bought for Ma, before she was a rebellious teenager, was still there. She touched the embroidered pattern of flowers before opening the box. *Ma liked flowers.* Inside was her favourite blue sapphire ring, as well as different earrings. She pulled the ring from the green felt backing, adjusted it and put it on her finger. Ma had said she had it made so that she could adjust it to fit her, but Emily had never seen other rings like this, other than ones you get out of a gumball machine. She stared at the egg shaped jewel. It sparkled like the sun dancing on the blue waters of the ocean. *Can't be real.* Ma said it was, but she never believed her.

"Hello," a voice called from below.

"I'm up here." She turned and called.

Auntie Sue came up the stairs and walked up to her. "Ah, you are looking at your mother's jewelry," she said and smiled.

"What do you think?" Emily asked showing her aunt the ring.

"Yes, that is a very old style ring. Your Ma had that made long time ago!"

"Is it real?" she asked.

"Yes! Yes, of course, it is!"

"Are you sure? It's almost too bright to be a real one, don't you think?"

"What?" Auntie Sue narrowed her eyes and started to laugh.

Emily watched her aunt cover her mouth, but still the giggling sounds erupted.

"Ai...so funny," Auntie Sue choked out.

Emily started to smile. "What?"

"Your...your face." Her aunt pointed at her, clutched at her stomach, laughing still more.

She turned to face the mirror and saw her pout. *Oh my God! What am I doing?* She turned away horrified, but Auntie's Sue's laugh was infectious. *I looked like Ma!* A small chortle escaped her, followed by a ripple of louder giggles. She never thought she was like her mother, but maybe she was. That might explain her crazy behaviour the other day too. Accusations and guilt tripping – wasn't that just like Ma? Soon Emily was wiping her eyes, and she exhaled to catch her breath. It was funny, the similarities in their facial expressions, but she never wanted to act like her mother again!

"Ai Emily," Auntie Sue said as she pulled her close.

She held her aunt for a few minutes. They never laughed like this, she and Ma. Never.

"Look under here," her aunt said removing the top layer of the jewelry box. "This jade necklace, your Ma wants you to have when you get married." She said holding up a white gold jade necklace with six jade pieces, and a jade centrepiece hanging down.

"Really?" she said.

"Yes and this bracelet," her aunt said showing her the set. "Your Ma bought it for you in Hong Kong before you were born!"

Emily placed the necklace round her neck and hooked the jade bracelet on. "What do you think?" she asked as she looked at herself in the mirror.

"Ah, very beautiful," Auntie Sue said with a smile.

She touched the cold metal and looked at the bright green of the jade against her skin. She never cared for the look of jade. No one else wore jade or real gold necklaces in school, although real gold necklaces and dog tags came into vogue when she was a teenager. She also knew that Chinese brides often wore lots of jade and gold jewelry when they changed out of their wedding dress into their cheongsam. A lump started to grow in her throat and she felt her eyes welling up. *Where will Ma be?* She looked down and quickly removed the jewelry.

"What's wrong?" Auntie Sue asked.

She shook her head, not wanting to upset her aunt and put the jewelry box away.

"Let's go downstairs," she said, taking her aunt's hand. As they descended the stairs, the front door open, and Sam walked in.

"Hey," he said to her before greeting Auntie Sue.

She was pleased to see him. "So what did you get us for lunch?" she asked as she realized she was starving.

"Just some subs," he said holding up the plastic bag.

"Hungry Auntie Sue?" she asked.

"I ate some food before I came over. You two eat."

They walked into the kitchen and took adjacent seats to each other at the kitchen table.

"What kind do you want?" he asked as he removed three subs from the bag. "I have assorted, roast beef and turkey."

"Let's share some," she suggested.

"Okay," he said as they each took half of the assorted sub and half of the roast beef.

She took a bite of the large sandwich, chewing down the raw onions, luncheon meats and vegetables. It tasted good, and she hungrily ate some more.

"Good," Auntie Sue said as she walked in. "You're both eating."

They ate silently with Auntie Sue watching. When they were done, Emily put the remaining submarine into the fridge.

"So," she said, "now what?" She was getting anxious to return to the hospital, even though she hadn't heard back from Dr. Lee.

"It's almost one o'clock," Sam said as he looked at his watch. "What time do you want to go back to the hospital?"

"Soon," Auntie Sue responded.

Emily nodded her head. "Maybe now?" She tried to sound nonchalant.

"Okay," Auntie Sue agreed. "I think your uncle is going to come too. I'll call him now."

"Great," Emily said. Dr. Lee should almost be done, she thought to herself as she wiped up the table. She joined Auntie Sue in the living room afterward, leaving Sam with his newspaper. She sat down beside her on the leather couch and grabbed her aunt's hand.

"I called your uncle," she said. "He is coming over now to take me to the hospital."

"Okay," she said softly.

"Your Ma was over there," Auntie Sue said pointing to the area in front of the coffee table. "I tried to help her..." she said as she started to cry.

"I know you did," Emily said as her eyes burned with tears. She held her aunt tightly, breathing hard.

"She didn't complain. She never said anything was wrong until she tried to go to the washroom. And then...and then, she just fell," Auntie Sue sobbed.

Emily felt an ache in her chest, and her throat constricted as she tried to control her convulsions.

Sam observed them, but kept a respectful distance away. She was thankful for his support.

The doorbell rang.

"It's your uncle," Auntie Sue said, as she wiped her eyes and grabbed some tissue to blow her nose.

"I'll open the door for him," Sam said leaping towards the front door.

Auntie Sue got up and walked to the hallway to meet her husband. "Are you ready to go?" she asked.

Emily had just finished blowing her nose as she emerged from the living room. "Hi, Uncle Henry," she said with a wave. Then she introduced Sam to her uncle. "Why don't you guys go first? I have one more phone call to make, so we can just meet you there."

Her aunt and uncle agreed and went ahead to the hospital. Emily raced back to the living room, picked up the phone and dialed. She paced, as she looked at her watch and waited. It was now almost two o'clock -- *shouldn't he be finished by now?* Again the answering machine picked up. Emily slammed the phone down. *Dammit, where is that man?*

"Okay, let's go," she said to Sam as she grabbed her purse and jacket. She followed Sam out, locked the door and rushed to the car.

After visiting with Ma, they were again seated in the Family Meeting Room with Dr. Goldberg.

"The situation is not improving," he began. "In fact, while you were gone, we had to resuscitate her twice."

"What do you mean?" Auntie Sue asked.

"I mean that her heart stopped," he replied.

Code Blue, Code Blue. Emily remembered what she heard over the PA system when they were leaving. *Maybe we shouldn't have left?* Her heart drummed uncontrollably.

"What should we do?" asked Auntie Sue.

"I recommend," Dr. Goldberg said slowly, "letting her go. We don't know what kind of brain damage she has suffered at this point, and it appears unlikely that she will regain consciousness."

Emily thought of her Ma's chest rising and falling by the force of the compressor. She felt tears coming to her eyes, as her mind raced. *How could this be happening?*

"I'm sorry," her aunt cried looking at her. "I'm sorry, Emily. We can't save her...we can't save her."

Tears erupted from her eyes now, and she fought to keep from exploding in front of this stranger. *This can't be happening? Wasn't Dr. Lee saving her?*

"Emily," Dr. Goldberg said, "is it okay for us to take your mom off of life support?"

She stared hard through her tears. *Ma?* She dug her nails into her hand to see if she was awake. *Ouch!* She was and she cried some more.

"We will give you some private time alone to say goodbye to her," Dr. Goldberg reassured them, "before we let her go."

As she studied Dr. Goldberg's face, her heart ached with a strange empty feeling. Suddenly more tears poured out of her, as she gasped for air. *No!* She looked at the doctor. He had already closed his file. Ma was gone.

"Emily?" Dr. Goldberg repeated.

She opened her mouth and swallowed. "Okay."

Dr. Goldberg nodded, got up and left the room. Auntie Sue cried loudly as she and Uncle Henry walked out.

Sam helped Emily out of her chair. Her legs felt weak. She leaned against him. She couldn't walk straight.

Auntie Sue and Uncle Henry stood first in front of Ma. Her aunt held Ma's hand and stood straight. "You can rest now. There's no more work to do," she said.

Emily stared in a daze. She was in a dream. *A bad dream.*

"You were a good mother, a good wife and," her aunt said, "the be...best sister. Rest now. Go. Be at peace." Her aunt kissed Ma and walked away.

Emily shuffled forward with Sam to Ma's bedside. Sam moved back a few steps to give her space. She stared at the pale, lifeless face. She saw Ma smiling, laughing, angry, pouting. *This can't be happening.* She placed Ma's small hand in hers. It was warm and she leaned down to pull it into her thudding chest. *Ma. Ma.* Her eyes clouded over. Was she really gone? She looked like she was sleeping. Maybe there's been a mistake? She heard someone cough and she jerked up. Suddenly her mind emptied and she saw her aunt, uncle and Sam were waiting for her. She felt numb like she was separated from her own body. *What do I do?* Instead of feeling panic, she watched herself let her mother go. "Goodbye, Ma," she finally blurted out. She bent down and kissed her cheek. Sam said goodbye as well and the two of them stood back from the bed.

A nurse came in as if on cue, turned the compressor off and removed the facemask from her mother. Immediately, a straight line registered on the heart monitor, and the nurse quickly turned it off.

Ma let out a finally breath, and Auntie Sue motioned Emily and Sam move clear.

"Spirit," she said.

Emily looked up and wondered where Ma was going to now. She took Sam's outstretched hand and waited. Silently, they walked out of the room.

Chapter Eighteen

"Hi," Emily said as on her cell phone, as she drove home from work.

"Are you done?" Sam asked.

"Yeah, I'm just on my way home now. And you?"

"I'll be finished early today, so you want me to pick up dinner?" he asked

"Sure."

"Okay. You feel like Thai tonight?"

"Sounds good," she said.

"Okay, see you around 5:30," said Sam and he hung up.

Emily shut her cell phone off and turned down the driveway. She cranked the window down to unlock the underground garage door and drove in. Up the stairs she walked until she reached her apartment door.

Long day. Opening the door, she lumbered in, letting the heavily weighted briefcase straining her neck fall freely to the ground.

Inside, Emily kicked off her shoes and took a hanger out of the hallway closet and smiled. *Sam's scent.* Sam's clothes had taken up more room than she had expected and they had to hang some of his suits in the coat closet. She pushed her jacket in and closed the door. She walked into the bedroom.

The duvet and sheets had been pulled over the bed quickly this morning, as they were both running late. She pulled at the messy bedding to smooth it out and sat down to change. She glanced at her reflection in the mirror from the dark brown bureau and saw the heart shaped green object around her neck. She got up and moved closer, as her fingers touched the smooth green stone. *Ma.* Auntie Sue had given her this necklace at lunch last week. She told her that her mother had worn it when she was a young woman living in Hong Kong. Ma wore jade all her life. She told her it was for luck and prosperity. Emily never really cared for jade or believed in it. *Look what happened to Ma.* Oddly, she found herself drawn to the cold, green stone and wore it every day. A *piece of Ma?* She let the lifeless rock drop back against her clavicle and walked down the hall. Grabbing the remote, she turned the television on before settling down on the couch. A repeat episode of *Star Trek: The Next Generation* attracted her attention, and she put her feet up on the antique blanket box to watch.

Sam's television was much larger and more enjoyable than her old one was. She also liked his brown leather couch, as it was more comfortable than her green couch was. Her couch, bed and dining room table were donated when Sam moved in four weeks ago. It was his idea. After spending every night at her place after her mother died, he just suggested he move in one night. She was surprised and thrilled with the idea. Other things that they had duplicates of, they put in the storage room in the basement although it took a bit of discussion to decide whose items to put into storage. Sam seemed to have newer things, whereas Emily had hand-me-downs, along with some recently adopted items from her mother's house.

Emily sighed as she thought about her parents' home. She didn't really want any of the furniture, but Auntie Sue was determined to keep it. "It's in good shape, you should keep this," she had urged repeatedly as they looked around the house a month after Ma had died. She recalled their discussion.

"But Auntie Sue, I have no place to store all of this," she said.

"You will buy a house someday, right?" her aunt asked.

She nodded.

"You can store the furniture in my house after this house is sold," she said decidedly.

"Why don't you take what you like?" Emily asked hopefully.

"No, no," her aunt replied.

"I insist," Emily said strongly. "Please. If you like these leather couches and chair, take them. Ma would be pleased they are not being wasted, covered up in plastic in your basement."

Her aunt thought in silence for a few minutes. "You are right, Emily," she finally said. "Your mother would not be happy if we just wasted her things."

"That settles it then. Let's decide what you could use or want of Ma's, what we could donate, you know because it is just too old, and what I will save for myself."

Auntie Sue nodded and they started the long process of going through the whole house. She had taken a couple of weeks off work, thinking this would be more than adequate time to clean out the house. It took almost a month to get through everything! Emily even came across her own schoolbooks, notes, cards and clothing she had not looked at since she moved out.

One day while they were cleaning, she was surprised when a real estate agent knocked at the door. The agent told her she had a client who was interested in a home in her area. Emily had already decided to sell the house, since she had no desire to live in Oakville again. She let the agent inspect the whole house that day and was thrilled when the agent wanted to return the next day, Sunday, with her clients. Emily and Auntie Sue rushed about scrubbing, cleaning, throwing out garbage and trying to move furniture out. Worried about the smells of garlic and Chinese cooking that couldn't be cleaned away, Emily plugged in air fresheners in "sunny lemon" in all the rooms, an hour before the buyers arrived. Although her trick worked and she received a very reasonable offer on the house, she found herself wandering aimlessly through the rooms for the remainder of that day. In her old bed that night, she noticed a familiar smell and dreamed about Ma cooking soup downstairs in the stove. Although she didn't know how to make any of Ma's soups, Emily decided to bring her mother's soup pots, cooking utensils and soup ingredients home with her to Toronto.

During a television commercial, Emily got up and went to the kitchen for some juice. Her stomach growled, so she opened the pantry to find a snack. She kind of wanted soup and moved down the shelves looking for something suitable. When she got to the bottom shelf, she noticed some brown paper bags and took one out. A medicinal smell sprung from the bags and she scrunched up her nose in disgust. "Oh! Dr. Lee's herbs!" she groaned. She had stored the remaining herbs from Ma's treatment here.

"Stupid crap!" She grabbed the four bags incensed. Three were filled with Chinese herbs and the fourth one had pills that Ma took every day. *Dr. Lee. Dr. Lee.* She finally did hear back from that man, but not until Sunday, one day after she died. *Too little, too late!* She stuffed the medicine and herbs into a plastic grocery bag. "I'm going to get rid of these today!" she said as she grabbed her purse and headed out the door.

243

She picked up her cell phone and dialed Sam from the car.

"Hello?"

"Hi, Hon," she said. "Listen, I have an errand to run so I might be a bit late getting back."

"Oh," he said surprised. "I was going to call you too 'cause I have to finish something up for a client. Do you still want me to pick up the food?"

"Sure, I'll be back by six at the latest."

"Okay...I should be home around 6:30. What's up anyways?"

"Umm..." She looked down at the bags of herbs. "I'll talk to you about it later, okay?" she said as stepped down on the accelerator.

"All right," he said slowly.

"Bye," she said hanging up. She didn't want to get into it. Every time she talked about Dr. Lee with Sam, she got upset. *Why didn't he call back earlier? Maybe he could have helped?* When Sam asked her how Dr. Lee could have helped, she didn't know. He told her to forget about it. She couldn't.

She drove quickly, reached Main Street and turned south down a side road to park in the residential area. Her pace was swift, with arms held in tight across her chest. On the phone, all Dr. Lee could say was that he was sorry when he called. *That was it?* She was too upset to say anything more, so they left it at that. The bag she carried bounced off her left leg, creating a rhythmic rustling sound. She glanced at her watch. It was almost five o'clock when she crossed the road to reach his clinic. Inside, a single patient was waiting. The familiar smell of herbs that reminded Emily of marijuana welcomed her, and she took her usual seat on the tired furniture that lined the waiting room. Emily smiled at the woman waiting, but then quickly grabbed a magazine. That woman had known her mother. She had been in the office on days Emily visited her mother during treatment. Emily could feel her eyes looking in her direction. *Please don't ask.*

Suddenly the glass office door flew open and Dr. Lee walked out. Emily shot up, adrenaline racing. Dr. Lee simply smiled and motioned for her to sit.

"Justa few minutes, I hava some more patients, okay?" he said in his heavily accented English. Emily watched as Dr. Lee returned to his office to grab a handful of needles. He turned quickly on his heels and marched down the hall into a treatment room. *What should I do?* She wondered as she watched the tail of his lab coat disappear. Unexpectedly, her mother's smiling face appeared before her. She saw her mother crying, eating, pouting and lying in her casket. *Not here!* Emily leapt to her feet and pulled open the office door. She ran down the hall, plastic bag jiggling and into the washroom. Hot tears had already spilled down her cheeks and she crumbled down onto the toilet. Just a few months ago, her mother was having treatment here. Ma was getting stronger after only four weeks of treatment. Ma said she wanted to take a trip! She was sure Dr. Lee's treatment was going to save her. Didn't he cure a patient with bone cancer in the past? She saw herself calling and calling Dr. Lee the day Ma was dying in the hospital. *Why couldn't he save her? Did I do enough?* She heard herself moan. Dr. Eng's smiling face flashed through her mind. *That wretched man! Why didn't we change family doctors after Dad died?* Louder moans as her body started to shake and shudder. She covered her mouth. *Not here...*

Someone knocked on the door. "Emily, please comea out." It was Dr. Lee.

Emily tried to calm herself, but more tears exploded like lava running down a volcano. After what felt like hours, the crying finally subsided, and she wiped away the remaining streaks from her face. Another knock at the door. "Okay," she answered in a shaky voice. She grabbed at the small porcelain sink and pulled herself up. Bloodshot eyes stared back at her in the bathroom mirror. She turned on the facet, rinsed with some cold water, wiped, then pulled at the toilet roll to blow her nose until there was no more tissue. Slowly, labouringly she picked up her belongings and walked out of the washroom. Dr. Lee took Emily's arm and guided her into a chair in his office. She slumped back. Her purse and bag dropped to the ground. Dr. Lee closed the door.

Piles of patient folders were scattered across Dr. Lee's desk. Emily looked at the brown heap. No files had numbers or distinguishing codes.

Where was Ma's file now? She looked up at Dr. Lee, seated across from her. His eyes looked dull, his hair was unkempt and the lines in his face looked more pronounced than usual. She straightened up. She used to marvel at his youthful appearance, and she recalled how he would always smile and whisper to her, "It's the Chi." Life energy. *Where is it now?* She wrinkled her brow.

"What happened a Emily?" he asked concerned.

"You know," she said a bit confused. "Ma died eight weeks ago." Pressure was mounting between her eyes. She rubbed at it. "Remember? I called you on a Saturday and left you messages. You called me back on the Sunday, after Ma died." She tried to focus on his face, but he looked down at the desk.

"Emily, I'm a sorry...we couldn't save her," Dr. Lee said quietly after a few minutes. He stared back. His eyes looked wide. Tired.

She blinked. *He's sorry?* She wanted to ask him why he hadn't called back that Saturday. But she couldn't. *Be polite.* Ma was in her head. Instead, she heard herself say, "I know...it's not your...well, you tried your best." The dull pain moved behind her eyes. "Um...here are the leftover herbs and pills," she said pulling the bag off the ground. She put it on his desk. She had researched the properties of these special pills he had ordered from California. Nothing was said about cancer-curing properties, even though Dr. Lee said they would help. She watched Dr. Lee as he peered into the bag.

"Don't a worry," he said. "I'll count everything and pay you back."

Emily nodded, gaze fixed.

"I didn't know she would go so fast," added Dr. Lee.

Emily started. *What did he say?* Some patients thought Dr. Lee had psychic, maybe even mystical healing powers. Maybe she secretly believed this too?

When she worked at the clinic after university, she was skeptical about Chinese medicine. She really only took the job because she needed the work and had to kill time until her real job started. People from all walks of life came in – artsy types, rich and poor, young and old. Few of these individuals were actually Chinese, which surprised Emily. She expected to see grandmothers, fresh-off-the-boat types and not educated, worldly WASPY people. They taught her about Dr. Lee and what a great healer he was. Emily tried to remain objective. Maybe there was a scientific explanation for this. Secretly, she felt proud of his achievements. Your regular doctor or specialist can't help you, so you come here and get results! Not everyone got what they wanted. Some were scared away by the needles and the stinky herbs. In some strange way, working with Dr. Lee made her feel a little bit better about being Chinese and prideful that we had secret ways to cure or alleviate aliments. *She was a fool.* What about those disgruntled clients? The ones who disappeared after a couple of weeks of treatment. Dr. Lee always had his explanation for why it didn't work, but maybe the truth was he didn't have Godly powers and couldn't fix everything.

Her head had started to throb. She sucked in some air and gazed at the person across from her. *He's just a man.*

"Uh...I guess no one did," she said tentatively.

"If I could have helped more, I would have," replied Dr. Lee.

Emily looked away. Dr. Lee was talking, but she stared past him at the gold-framed picture of his young son behind him on a metal filing cabinet. The boy was sitting, holding a red balloon, smiling. He looked happy. Healthy. *What would you have done for him?* Suddenly she realized Dr. Lee had stopped talking.

"Well..." she said a bit aggressively. "I guess...I guess there's not much we can do now," she said as she stood abruptly up.

Dr. Lee came around his desk to her. Emily offered him her hand, but he pulled her towards him and gave her a hug. She stood stone like against his body, patted his arms awkwardly before pushing away.

"Goodbye," she said impatient to get out.

Emily walked out of the office. She glanced at the woman who was still seated in the waiting room. *Should she offer her some advice?* The woman looked away and lowered her head. Emily continued through the front door and made her way back to her vehicle.

Safely in her car, she pulled away. She felt exhausted. Something tickled her nose and she rolled down the window to air out the strange smells. *Chinese herbs.* She drove under the speed limit home. Her head cleared as she breathed in the early dusk air. It took her ten extra minutes to reach home. Parked underground, she walked up the stairs and headed out the front door of the apartment building. She stopped to look at the spring tulips. Their faces were receding, soon to be hidden for sleep. *Ma loved flowers.* "Good night," she said as she touched a yellow tulip and headed inside. Emily didn't bother with the lights in her apartment. She paused at the kitchen phone as she noticed Dr. Lee's crumpled looking business card. She picked it up and dropped it into a waste paper basket on her way to the living room.

About The Author

Anna Woo was first published in 1993 in a collection of short stories called Sharing our Experience, compiled by the Canadian Advisory Council on the Status of Women.

She has a Master Degree in Education in Counselling Psychology from the University of Toronto/Ontario Institute for Studies in Education (1997). In 2002, she completed the Creative Writing program through The Humber School for Writers.

Her Mother's Voice is her first fictional novel.

ACKNOWLEDGEMENTS

In 2000, I enrolled in a course in writing short stories at the University of Toronto with Kent Nussey. This is when my fictional writing really began, and I found inspiration studying with him. I wrote more and pursued more studies, completing the Creative Writing program through The Humber School for Writers in 2002 with Olive Senior as my mentor. My manuscript began to take shape during that process. I then had my manuscript reviewed by Sarah Sheard in 2007, and I also attended a writers group facilitated by her. Sarah's comments gave me the courage to continue working on this book.

After much editing and re-editing, I had the story reviewed by my friend Kelly Lamb, who also copy-edited the final draft. Her feedback and sharp editing skills gave me the confidence to publish this book. Thank you, Kelly.